BEAR WITH ME - 2023

An Ursine Dissection of the Politics, Societal Issues and Shenanigans of the United Kingdom

Iratus Ursus Major

This book is a work of non-fiction. While all efforts have been made to ensure accuracy and adherence to factual reporting, the views, opinions, and analyses expressed herein are solely those of the author. They do not necessarily represent the views of any other person or entity.

To my husband, who has endured my rants, tolerated my eccentricities, and still manages to look at me with a straight face.

Your patience is legendary, and my luck is borderline unfair.

Here's to you.

DEAR SANDRA,

THANK YOU SO MUCH FOR YOUR SUPPORT

ALL THE BEST,

In a time of deceit, telling the truth is a revolutionary act.

GEORGE ORWELL

INTRODUCTION

Well, here it is – "Bear With Me - 2023." If you told me a year ago that I'd be compiling a book, I'd have laughed you out of the room – and then probably written a scathing tweet about your wild optimism. But life's strange like that, isn't it?

First and foremost, a gargantuan thank you to my husband. You've not only put up with my incessant typing and muttering but also managed to feign interest in my late-night ramblings about politics and social injustices. Saint? Masochist? Both? Either way, you're the bedrock of this unlikely literary adventure.

And to my followers on Substack and Twitter, you are all the true heroes here. Since that fateful July 2023, you've turned my small internet corner into a bustling hub of debate and discussion. Your enthusiasm for my posts on the government's latest shenanigans, the climate crisis, and the absolute circus of modern politics has been overwhelming and slightly terrifying.

You've transformed my rants on LGBTQ rights, the absurdities of Brexit, and the never-ending saga of social inequality into something resembling a movement. I'm still unsure how you did it, but here we are.

If I'm being brutally honest, this whole book thing feels a bit like a vanity project. There's a nagging voice in my head telling me I'm just an imposter with a keyboard. But, if there's one thing I've learned, sometimes you must embrace the cringe and roll with it.

So, to everyone who's believed in the angry rants of a self-proclaimed 'Big Angry Bear' – thank you from the bottom of my heart. Your support has been both humbling and invigorating.

Strap in, folks. This isn't just a book; it's a compilation of thoughts, tweets, and essays that have resonated with many brilliant people. It's raw, unapologetic, and as subtle as a bear at a tea party. Let's dive into the madness that was 2023 – a year that somehow turned a grumbling cynic into an accidental author.

TABLE OF CONTENTS

NOTABLE TWITTER POSTS

LONG FORM WRITING AND ESSAYS

A Collection of Long Form Posts and Essays Published in 2023

THE BEAR BEHIND THE WORDS AND THE MILESTONE OF MADNESS

(Author's Note: This piece was written at the point at which I reached 100 subscribers on Substack. I've kept the piece completely intact as I feel it conveys the sense of excitement and astonishment that I felt, as well as just how grateful I was for the amazing number of people who had followed me at that point. I still feel this way.)

Well, isn't this a peculiar predicament? Here stands a man, more bear than human, armed with nothing but a penchant for profanity, ready to delve deep into the depths of his digital domain. Why, you ask? An astonishing 115 brave souls have subscribed to my Substack, not to mention the 8,000 followers on Twitter who've decided to hop aboard this crazy train. If that's not a reason for a little celebration (and introspection), I'm not sure what is.

It's quite the surreal sensation, realising that people - actual living, breathing humans - find my tirades against the Tories and my vehement verbosity enjoyable rather than unbearable. It's like discovering your secret collection of vintage sporks is suddenly in vogue. Baffling, indeed, but who am I to complain?

Now, as we stand on the brink of personal revelation, I can't help but feel like I'm at the edge of a precipice, shouting into the abyss and hoping not to sound like a complete twatwaffle. But for the sake of camaraderie, curiosity, and our collective disdain for governmental incompetence, I'm ready to take the plunge.

(Have I mentioned just how hard I'm cringing at the moment just writing this? I've always hated talking about myself, and this is absolutely no exception)

So, let's give this a go. I'm Iratus, the Angry Bear of the internet, the digital dissenter who finds solace in calling out calamity and corruption. But who is the human behind the moniker? What led to the creation of this cantankerous character of the web?

In the chapter that follows, I'll peel back the oniony layers, exploring everything from my bear-like physique and boundless love for tech to my journey as a polyglot migrant. We'll traverse the tumultuous terrain of public health, my day job and major source of stress, and we'll discover the passions and principles that fuel my prolific posts.

So, grab your snack of choice, settle into your comfiest chair, and prepare for a deep dive into the peculiar world of Iratus Ursus. It's bound to be a wild, weird, and wordy journey. And remember, we maintain a strict no-shitgibbon policy here. We keep it real, raw, and irreverently honest. Welcome, dear reader, to the Bear's Den.

A Linguistic Labyrinth: My Multilingual Melee

As the digital confetti settles in the intervoid, marking the milestone of reaching over 100 subscribers interested in my mad ramblings, I find myself reflecting on my linguistic journey.

How did I, a bear of a man from a land where English was more of a tourist than a resident, end up wielding it as my weapon of choice in the relentless battle against political absurdity?

From an early age, I found myself juggling languages like a circus performer, with English being one of the more demanding balls in the air. It wasn't the language of my home or my streets, but it was the language of my books, my shows, and my inner monologues when I felt particularly theatrical. It was a relationship built on curiosity and a love for the dramatic rather than necessity.

Navigating the nuances of English while surrounded by a sea of other linguistic influences was nothing short of a wild ride. Imagine learning ballet, only to be interrupted by spontaneous urges to breakdance - that was my experience with English. It was a love affair with a language that was as exasperating as it was enchanting, and I was all in.

I revelled in its quirks, danced with its irregular verbs, and had fiery debates with its nonsensical rules ('i' before 'e' except after 'c'—really?). English became my secret sanctuary, my playground, and my battlefield – and one that I got roundly mocked for because it is not at all a popular language in my homeland.

This linguistic labyrinth has bestowed upon me a voice that is unmistakably mine - accented, quirky, and unabashedly pissed off. English has enabled me to dissect the political circus, unleash my inner wordsmith on unsuspecting fools, and find solace amidst the chaos. It has become my sword and shield, my ally in the war of words, and my ticket to a community of fellow rant enthusiasts.

Though I may be a migrant and a second-language English speaker, English has become my scalpel, my instrument of precision in the dissection of political absurdities. I wield it with a blend of delight and vengeance, a bear armed with a keyboard, a cup of tea, and a vendetta against political nonsense.

The Bear Behind The Keyboard: A Gentle Giant's Crusade Against B.s.

Now, venturing deeper into the bear's lair, you might be wondering what drives a man of my stature to type away his grievances furiously. Picture a 6ft3 fortress of a man, built like a (slightly squidgy) brick shithouse, beard as black as my coffee and streaked with strands of distinguished (or not) grey.

I'm your quintessential gentle giant, a retired rugby player who's traded scrums for words. My friends, family, and my ever-patient husband of 13 years (yes, I've mentioned him before, but he deserves another shoutout for putting up with me) would all attest to my "big teddy bear" demeanour. But beneath this amiable exterior beats a heart passionate about justice and standing up for what's right.

So, why the furious typing, you might ask? It's my solace, my stressbuster, my community, and my platform to shout "SHITGIBBON" at the top of my digital lungs. My day job in public health is rewarding, but it's like solving a Rubik's cube while blindfolded - stressful is putting it mildly.

I find myself here, writing, venting, and bearing (pun intended) my soul to the world. The keyboard is my weapon, and words are my ammunition. In the wild west of the internet, where misinformation spreads like wildfire, I've taken it upon myself to be the Bear with a hose, ready to extinguish the flames of falsehoods and call out the bullshit.

And you, my dear readers, have become my posse, rallying around me, sharing in my rants, and finding amusement in my artful use of expletives. It's a camaraderie I never expected but am profoundly grateful for.

As I embark on this new chapter, dedicating a day a week to writing and inching closer to making this my main gig, I do so with a heart brimming with thanks. It's a peculiar journey we're on, but it's ours, and the bear in me is overjoyed to have you along for the ride.

A Bear's Bumbling Beliefs

If, by some miracle of patience or a peculiar penchant for punishment, you've made it this far, I extend to you my most heartfelt and bewildered thanks. You're still here? Well, buckle up because the bear is about to bare his soul (yes, the pun is, again, intentional, and no, I'm not apologising).

Now, I'd love to claim that my relentless tirades and passionate prose are the result of a well-thought-out philosophical stance, but let's be honest - I'm winging it. Nevertheless, there are a few convictions that fuel my fervour.

Politics is not just a pastime; it's an all-consuming blaze and has become my sport. I'm utterly captivated by the pursuit of holding the powerful accountable, ensuring justice is more than just an ideal, and shouting "SHITGIBBON" at anyone who dares to corrupt the system. I dream of a world where fairness is a given, irrespective of one's background, beliefs, or whom one chooses to love.

On immigration, as a seasoned migrant and spouse (yes, there's that 13-year marriage again), I've experienced the highs and lows of finding a home in a new place. From visa nightmares to the joy of discovering new communities, I've navigated the bittersweet journey of belonging and otherness.

LGBTQ rights? Absolutely. Having tied the knot with my husband before it was widely accepted (and let's face it, it's sadly still not completely), I stand firmly with the LGBTQ community, T included. We're all navigating this tumultuous world together, and no one gets left behind.

And then there's my tumultuous love affair with language. It's a wild, passionate, and utterly ridiculous relationship. I delight in crafting sentences sharp enough to cut through political drivel and colourful enough to make a sailor blush. My vocabulary is a chaotic playground, and I'm the mischievous child with a spray can.

But let's be clear - I'm not some noble keyboard warrior with an unblemished moral compass. I'm flawed, I'm fumbling, and I'm typing furiously in the hope of making even the smallest dent in the world's absurdities.

As I navigate this chaotic journey of political discourse, remember that this is more than just a venting session. It's a clumsy, chaotic crusade. I may not have all the answers (or any, really), but I've got plenty of questions and a keyboard that's not afraid to ask them.

With every post, rant, and creatively chosen expletive, I'm stumbling toward a world that's just a bit fairer, a touch kinder, and a whole lot less tolerant of nonsense. And if you've made it this far, well, you're probably stumbling right along with me.

A Bear's Aspirations And Acknowledgments

As we reach the culmination of this labyrinthine journey through the convoluted corridors of my conscience, I find myself oscillating between sentimentality and sheer astonishment. Have I really just laid bare the inner workings of my bearish brain for the entire internet to see? It seems I have.

Here I am (or rather, sitting with a hunched back and in dire need of a better ergonomic chair) at a crossroads in my digital diatribes. With a heart overflowing with gratitude and a MacBook on its last legs, I take a moment to both reflect and project.

This writing endeavour began as a form of stress relief, a way to shout into the void about a world seemingly gone mad. It was my digital scream into a pillow, a means of coping with the colossal craziness of modern politics.

Yet, as time marched on, something extraordinary happened. I discovered you - a community of like-minded, slightly mad individuals ready to embrace an angry bear and join in this journey of collective catharsis. Together, we've laughed, ranted, and navigated the tumultuous seas of Twitter (and now potentially Substack once I figure out how it all works), all while mostly keeping our sense of humour intact.

Now, with a hundred subscribers on Substack (a number I still can't quite wrap my head around) and a renewed commitment to dedicate a day a week to writing, I find myself daring to dream. Could this venting platform transform into a viable career? Could the bear with a penchant for profanity and a love for linguistic lunacy actually turn this into a living along with my day job?

The future is as uncertain as a British weather forecast, but one thing is crystal clear - I'm eager to give it my best shot. With every post, rant, and creative expletive, I'm inching closer to a life where public health stress takes a back seat, and the joy of writing drives the journey.

So, here's to the adventure, the insanity, and the 115 subscribers who've chosen to endure my bearish babbling. I'm awestruck, I'm grateful, and I'm slightly concerned about your taste in reading material. But above all, I'm thrilled - thrilled for what lies ahead, for the community we're building, and for the opportunity to turn this passion into something more.

Thank you, from the deepest caverns of my bearish heart, for joining me on this wild, weird, and wordy ride. The path forward is fraught with uncertainty; the typos are bound to continue, but the journey. It promises to be anything but dull. Here's to the next chapter, the next rant, and the next 100 subscribers. May our words be plentiful, our spirits buoyant, and our tolerance for political nonsense perpetually low. Welcome to the den, dear reader - the bear is just getting started.

BOILING OVER: THE UK'S DESCENT INTO POLITICAL MADNESS

From Austerity to Brexit and Beyond: A No-Holds-Barred Look at How Britain's Political Landscape Turned Toxic

Alright, strap in, folks, because we're about to embark on a journey through the political swamp that's slowly been boiling us alive. Think of it as a grim fairy tale, except it's real, and the monsters are in suits.

We're living in an era that's more batshit crazy than a conspiracy theorist's wet dream. From the ashes of Austerity, birthed by the dubious duo of (the now Lord) Cameron and his sinister sidekick, Osborne, we've witnessed a gradual erosion of common decency and a leap into an Orwellian nightmare. It's like we've been slowly lulled into a state of complacency, numbed to the point where outrageous becomes the new normal.

It's not just about the economic screwing over - though let's face it, that's been like a masterclass in how to bankrupt a nation both morally and financially. It's about the brazen attack on basic human rights, cloaked in the flag and sold as policy. You've got the likes of Liz Truss, who seems to think workers' rights are about as important as a chocolate teapot, and Suella Braverman, who treats human decency like it's a game of Whack-A-Mole.

The recent cavalcade of Tory madness isn't just a series of unfortunate events; it's a calculated push towards a society where the rich get richer on the backs of the poor, and the vulnerable are left to fend for themselves in the cold. It's a world where compassion is a liability, and the only currency worth anything is power.

And as if that wasn't enough, we're now teetering on the edge of a legal precipice. The Tories are itching to rewrite the Human Rights Act and take a sledgehammer to the ECHR. Why? Nothing says

"Great Britain" like trampling over the rights of the least among us.

So, let's pull back the curtain and see how we got here. How did we go from "Keep Calm and Carry On" to "Fuck the Poor and Praise the Rich"? How did Austerity become the gateway drug to this current hellscape?

It's a tale of greed, of power, and of a slow descent into madness. And it's about time we started paying attention before the pot boils over, and we're left with nothing but ashes.

The Austerity Altar: Sacrificing The Poor For Political Gain

Let's rewind to the early 2010s, a period that now feels like a prequel to a dystopian novel. This was when Austerity, the brainchild of that dubious duo, Cameron and Osborne, began its grim and relentless march across the UK. It was sold to us as a necessary evil, a way to tighten our belts for the greater good. But let's call it what it was: a systematic dismantling of the welfare state, served with a side of scorn for anyone not wealthy enough to dodge the bullet.

Austerity wasn't just about cutting budgets; it was a cultural shift, a way to turn public opinion against those struggling the most. It was as if the government had declared open season on people with low incomes. Benefits? Slashed. Public services? Gutted. And all the while, the rich got tax breaks like they were going out of fashion.

This wasn't just economic policy; it was class warfare disguised as fiscal responsibility. It was like watching a reverse Robin Hood in action, only less charming and more destructive. We saw libraries close, mental health services crumble, and the NHS buckle under the strain – all in the name of "balancing the books". The government wasn't just cutting fat; they were hacking away at the very bone and sinew that hold up our society.

And the most tragic part? We bought into it. Millions along as the narrative was spun, painting people experiencing poverty as lazy, people with disabilities as scroungers, and immigrants as the root of all evil. It was a masterclass in divide and conquer, and it was lapped up by so many, many people like a cat with a bowl of cream.

But here's the crux: Austerity didn't just pave the way for economic hardship; it laid the groundwork for the current political fuckery we're living through right this moment. It desensitised us and made us more accepting of the unthinkable. It was like the proverbial boiling of a frog - slowly turn up the heat, and the poor amphibian won't even realise it's being cooked alive.

Fast forward to today, and we're reaping the whirlwind that Austerity sowed. The gap between the rich and the poor is not only a ravine; it's a chasm. Social mobility is a fairy tale that we tell ourselves, and our political discourse is more toxic than a vat of nuclear waste. Austerity wasn't just a policy; it was a gateway drug to the very hellscape we're living in now.

So, as we stare into the abyss of the current political landscape, remember this: it all started with Austerity. It was the first domino to fall, the spark that lit the fire. And now, we're all burning in the inferno of its legacy.

Brexit: The Leap From The Frying Pan Into The Fire

Now, let's take a detour into the Brexit saga, shall we? Because, let's face it, Brexit was the moment we went from the slow simmer of austerity to a full-on leap into the raging fire of unaccountability and governmental fuckery.

This wasn't just about leaving the EU; it was the first major step in severing ties with external accountability and moderation. It was like cutting off the referee's whistle in the middle of a football match and saying, "Right, let's just play without any bloody rules, shall we?"

The whole Brexit charade was sold to us under the banner of taking back control, but what it really did was give the Tories a free pass to run rampant. It was like opening Pandora's box and finding it stuffed with every right-wing wet dream imaginable. And boy, have they been living it up ever since.

With Brexit, our government took a sharp turn towards isolation, not just geographically but ideologically. It's like they suddenly felt emboldened to enact all sorts of madness without the pesky interference of European sensibilities. Think of it as the starting gun for the race to the bottom in terms of human rights, workers' rights, and common bloody decency.

The Brexit fallout is a clear marker of our descent into this Tory dystopia. It's the point where the mask slipped, revealing the true face of a government that's more interested in pandering to its base instincts than in safeguarding the rights and well-being of its citizens. It's like they've been given the keys to the kingdom and have decided to redecorate with a bulldozer.

In essence, Brexit was our first big dive into a world where our government suddenly became less accountable, not just to outside forces but to its own people. It's set the stage for all the madness we're seeing now - from the attacks on people with low incomes and the vulnerable to the outright assault on our human rights.

So, as we look at the current state of affairs, let's remember the role Brexit played in getting us here. It wasn't just a political decision; it was the catalyst for a seismic shift in our political landscape, one that's left us teetering on the edge of a very dangerous precipice.

Brexit might have been the leap, but it's up to us to ensure we don't land in a future where the very fabric of our society is torn to shreds by those who couldn't give a toss about anyone but themselves.

The Current Environment: A Playground For Political Pantomime

Jumping to the present of our current hellscape, where the legacy of Austerity has blossomed into a full-blown shitshow of political pantomime. The stage is set with characters who would be laughable if they weren't so damned dangerous. We've got Robert Jenrick playing arts and crafts with refugee centres, stripping them of any semblance of child-friendliness. It's like taking a Boeing engine to a house of cards and then wondering why it falls apart.

Then there's our now departed Suella Braverman, or as I fondly call her, Cruella. This woman has the compassion of a concrete slab with none of the utility. Describing homelessness as a *"lifestyle choice"* and wanting to criminalise tents? It's like watching a villain from a Dickens novel come to life, only more twisted and heartless. And let's not forget her cronies, echoing her vile sentiments like a gaggle of brain-dead parrots.

Enter Liz Truss with her economic wizardry that makes a drunk monkey look like Einstein—calling for the dismantling of workers' rights, slashing minimum wage, and attacking paid leave? It's like she's on a personal crusade to drag us back into the dark ages, one catastrophic policy at a time.

And then, the cherry on this dystopian cake: Rishi Sunak, our Prime Miniature, with his disdain for a ceasefire march on Armistice Day. It's like he's allergic to irony, and this is not even delving into his fire sale of our most dearly held rights to Cruella Braverman as his Faustian bargain for a little bit of power. His reign so far is like watching a man trying to put out a fire with a flamethrower - misguided, ineffective, and frankly, a little bit scary.

But let's not forget the supporting cast – Lee Anderson telling refugees to "fuck off", Jonathan Gullis existing in the August House of Commons, and a Tory candidate telling the poor to do one and then looking all sheepish that he did not in fact win a spot in Parliament. It's a line-up that would be hilarious in a satire, but tragically, this is real life.

This grotesque theatre of the absurd we're witnessing today is the direct offspring of the Austerity era. It normalised the abnormal, made the unthinkable thinkable, and turned the political landscape into a playground for the worst kind of opportunists.

The consequences? Dire. We've got 3.8 million people living in destitution, workers' rights hanging by a thread, and human rights about to be trampled under the jackboots of political expediency. It's like watching a speeding train in slow motion heading to a cliff, except we're all on the damned train, and no one can get to the conductor to stop his insane path of destruction.

We're at a crossroads, where the choice is stark: either we continue down this path of madness, or we stand up and say, "Enough is enough". The future of our society, our decency, and our very humanity depends on it.

On The Precipice Of Peril

As we teeter on the edge of this political precipice, let's talk about human rights – or, more accurately, the impending erosion thereof. If the current lot in charge have their way, we'll be waving goodbye to basic decency faster than a gambler's money on a bad night.

The Tories' lustful gaze at the prospect of rewriting the Human Rights Act and ditching the European Convention on Human Rights (ECHR) isn't just concerning; it's fucking terrifying. It's like handing a pyromaniac a flamethrower and asking them to babysit your garage full of fuel. The level of potential cruelty and injustice that could be unleashed is just staggering.

Take, for instance, Liz Truss's diabolical idea to dilute workers' rights. We're talking paid leave, minimum wage, redundancy pay - the whole nine yards. If the Tories get their way, these rights could be slashed with the abandon of a drunk butcher in a meat market. It's not just a rollback; it's a full-on assault on the working class.

Then there's the Rwanda scheme, a human rights violation so blatant it makes my blood boil, but which has just been ruled against by the Supreme Court. Shipping off asylum seekers like they're parcels? It's a policy so devoid of humanity, it could only have been dreamt up in the darkest recesses of a very twisted mind and should never have been tabled in our Parliament. Good riddance to it.

But let's not stop there. The potential consequences for marginalised and poorer communities are as severe as a kick in the teeth. We're looking at a future where the vulnerable are not just ignored but actively trampled upon. It's a dystopian vision that would make Orwell himself say, "Hold on, that's a bit much."

This isn't just a political debate; it's a battle for the soul of our nation. We're staring down the barrel of a future where human rights are a negotiable commodity, up for sale to the highest bidder or the loudest ideologue. It's a world where the powerful can crush the powerless under their heel without a second thought.

So, as we stand on this dangerous brink, it's time to ask ourselves: what kind of country do we want to be? Do we want to be a nation that protects the vulnerable and upholds basic human decency?

Or do we slide into the abyss of right-wing wet dreams where compassion is a weakness, and cruelty is government policy?

The answer, my friends, is as clear as a gin in a dirty glass. We fight. We fight against the erosion of our rights, the trampling of our values, and the descent into a heartless hellscape. This is a fight we can't afford to lose. Not just for ourselves, but for the very fabric of what makes us human.

Supreme Court Smackdown: A Double-Edged Sword

The UK Supreme Court has today lobbed a legal grenade into the lap of the government, blasting the Rwanda Scheme to smithereens. This decision is a monumental win for human rights, but it's also like ringing the dinner bell for the Tory's hard-line faction, itching to tear up the Human Rights Act and flip the bird to the ECHR.

Let's not delude ourselves, this isn't just about a failed scheme; it's like we've lit the fuse on a political powder keg. The ruling is a welcome slap in the face for those in power who thought they could play fast and loose with asylum seekers' lives. But for the right-wing crotchgoblins within the Tory party, it's a rallying cry to go full throttle on their crusade against what they see as pesky human rights laws getting in their way.

Rewriting the Human Rights Act? Bailing on the

ECHR? That's not just tweaking the rules; it's a full-blown demolition derby on our commitments to basic decency and fairness. We're talking about a shift that could see the UK go from a nation that respects rights to one that tramples them underfoot in the name of "control". And let's be real, if this ludicrous lot gets their way, the Rwanda Scheme will look like child's play compared to the draconian dystopia they'd love to usher in.

This isn't just about immigration policy; it's a battle for what kind of country we want to be. Do we stand up for rights and dignity, or do we let a bunch of power-hungry wankspangles turn the UK into a playground for their most heartless whims? The Supreme Court may have dealt a blow to the Rwanda Scheme, but the aftermath is setting the stage for a much bigger showdown - a clash over whether human rights are a cornerstone of our society or a mere inconvenience to be bulldozed when it suits the agenda of those in charge.

In short, the Supreme Court's decision is a double-edged sword. It's stopped one humanitarian horror show, but it's also potentially opened the floodgates for an onslaught against human rights that we'll be fighting tooth and nail. The stakes? They couldn't be bloody higher.

Standing at the Crossroads

Here we are then, standing at a crossroads, the

Supreme Court's decision on the Rwanda Scheme echoing like a thunderclap in the background. This isn't just about one failed policy; it's a symbol of the larger battle we're entrenched in. The question now isn't just what kind of country we've become, but what kind we're hell-bent on becoming.

The Tories, with their penchant for power at any cost, are poised on the precipice of a dangerous path. They're like kids in a candy store of cruelty, eyes glinting at the prospect of dismantling human rights protections and reshaping the UK into a playground for their most ruthless fantasies.

We've watched, almost in a stupor, as they've played fast and loose with the lives of the vulnerable. From Jenrick's heartless makeover of refugee centres to Braverman's diabolical tent ban, from Truss's callous crusade against workers' rights to Sunak's cold dismissal of calls for peace. Each step has been a lurch towards a darker, more divided Britain, where the rights and dignities of the many are sacrificed at the altar of the few.

The Supreme Court ruling is a beacon of hope, a reminder that there are still lines that can't be crossed. But it's also a stark warning - the forces arrayed against basic decency are not just at the gates; they're already inside, brandishing their torches with glee.

Brexit was our first giant leap into uncharted territory, a move away from external checks and balances. Now, with the Tories' newfound appetite for tearing up the Human Rights Act and ditching the ECHR, we're staring down the barrel of a future where the government's power is unchecked, and the vulnerable are left without a safety net.

As we brace for what's to come, let's remember: this is a marathon, not a sprint. The fight for a fair, just, and humane Britain is a long one, and we can't afford to lose steam. The Supreme Court's decision has given us a momentary reprieve, but the battle rages on. We need to stay vigilant, vocal, and utterly unyielding.

This is more than a political squabble; it's a clash of values, a struggle for the soul of our nation. Are we a country that stands up for the underdog, champions the cause of justice, and upholds the rights of all? Or do we slide into an abyss of callousness and cruelty, where might makes right, and compassion is a relic of the past?

The answer lies with us, the beleaguered, but unbroken, citizens of this increasingly surreal island. Our resolve, our outrage, our collective voice - these are the weapons in our arsenal. And by all that's holy, we're going to need them.

So, as we gear up for the next round in this never-ending political boxing match, let's remember what we're fighting for: a Britain that's kinder, fairer, and just a damn sight better than what these thunderwanks are trying to turn it into.

To the barricades, then. There's work to be done.

GOVERNMENTAL SHITSHOW UNMASKED: WHATSAPP REVELATIONS LAY BARE A CIRCUS OF INCOMPETENCE

Diving into the chaotic cesspool of leaked messages, we unravel the staggering levels of confusion and fuckery in Downing Street, igniting a fury and an unyielding call for accountability.

In the heart of a crisis that shook our nation to its core, the COVID Inquiry stands as a testament to our relentless pursuit of truth and accountability. It's a saga, a grand inquisition, laying bare the inner workings of a government that seemed to be playing a game of Russian roulette with the lives of millions. And at the centre of this storm are Martin Reynolds, Simon Case, and Lee Cain - key players in a drama that unveils the chaos and disarray of Boris Johnson's reign.

Reynolds, the man with the keys to the Prime Minister's office, found himself in the hot seat yesterday, his words and actions under the scrutiny of a nation demanding answers. Case, the top civil servant, emerges not just as a bystander, but a critical voice drowned out in a sea of indecision and ineptitude, but much worse still, through his silence an active collaborator. And Cain, the communications chief, holds pieces of this puzzle, his testimony eagerly anticipated, yet hanging in the balance as he did not arrive for his time in the limelight.

This inquiry is not just a reckoning; it's a mirror reflecting the broken pieces of a government that lost its way. It's a story of incendiary WhatsApp messages, of a Prime Minister's office that turned into a circus, with strategies changing as quickly as the British weather. It's a tale of regret, of apologies too late in the coming, and of cultural rot that permeated the hallowed halls of power when we needed compassionate adults in charge the most.

But let's not kid ourselves. This is also about accountability, about dissecting the hows and the whys, and ensuring that those responsible are not just named, but held to account. It's about making sure that the blunders, the missteps, and the outright failures of this government are laid bare for all to see.

So buckle up, because this is not just another political drama. This is a story of a nation, of lives lost and lessons painfully learned. And by God, it's about time we got some bloody answers.

The WhatsApp Exposé and a Government in Crisis

Diving into the tempestuous sea of these WhatsApp revelations, we find ourselves amidst a storm of discontent, frustration, and outright disbelief. Cummings, Case, and Cain, the architects of our discontent, have laid it all bare in their digital confessions, painting a vivid picture of a government spiralling out of control.

"Moronic." That's how Cummings describes his interactions with the ministers. Not just a throwaway comment, but a scathing indictment of those tasked with steering the ship during one of the most tumultuous times in recent history. They're clueless, utterly out of their depth, and seemingly oblivious to the magnitude of the crisis at hand.

"This is embarrassing," Cain adds, voicing the exasperation felt by many as we watched the government fumble and flounder. And Simon Case? He's right there, amidst the chaos, his messages brief yet loaded with frustration. "Spectacular," he remarks sarcastically, as Boris Johnson, the captain of this rudderless ship, changes course yet again, abandoning caution and embracing recklessness.

But Johnson isn't the only one in their line of fire. Oh no, Hancock, our then-Health Secretary, comes under scathing attack. "Joker," Cain asserts, cutting through the charade with a dose of brutal honesty. Hancock, it seems, had become the embodiment of the government's failings, a symbol of incompetence in a time that demanded decisiveness and clarity.

And let's not forget the original message from Simon Case that kicked off this whole sordid affair: "IT HAS TO STOP! Decide and set a direction - deliver - explain. Government isn't actually that hard, but this guy is really making it impossible." These words, raw and unfiltered, reveal a man at the end of his tether, a witness to the unfolding disaster, frustrated and disillusioned.

"We look like a terrible, tragic joke," Case confesses, laying bare the government's credibility crisis. The indecision, the flip-flopping, and the sheer incompetence have left us looking like the world's worst circus act, with Case and company relegated to the role of unwilling spectators.

As we sift through the digital debris of their conversations, what becomes abundantly clear is that we were failed. Failed by a government mired in chaos, failed by leaders too caught up in their own turmoil to see the iceberg ahead. And in the midst of this tragic farce, we are left with a sense of betrayal, anger, and an overwhelming desire for accountability.

The Human Aspect – Apologies, Regret, and Cultural Shitshow

As the WhatsApp shitstorm unfolded, the human aspect of this governmental farce came sharply into focus. Martin Reynolds, once the right-hand man to the Prime Minister, found himself in a whirlwind of conscience, spewing apologies that, while necessary, screamed of insincerity and desperation.

"Deeply sorry," he declared, his words echoing through the chambers of the inquiry like a hollow dirge. But let's call a spade a spade, shall we? Would this bout of remorse have reared its head if the inquiry hadn't ripped the veil off Downing Street's inner circus? Was this apology a heartfelt mea culpa, or just another calculated ploy in a game of damage control?

The inquiry ripped the mask off more than just individual failings; it exposed a cultural cesspit, a toxic brew of misogyny, neglect, and power plays. Women were treated like background noise, diversity was tossed aside like yesterday's rubbish, and the air was thick with the stench of arrogance. Reynolds, with a hint of reluctance in his voice, admitted as much. There was a cancer eating away at the heart of government, but as the ship of state lurched from one disaster to the next, these festering wounds were left to rot.

Enter Simon Case, Lee Cain, and Dominic Cummings – a trio caught in a digital dance of frustration and despair. Their WhatsApp exchanges laid it all bare: a government not just in disarray, but at war with itself. We, the public, were left to sift through the digital wreckage, finding a government stripped bare, its failures and flaws exposed for the world to see.

What were we left with? Apologies that tasted of bile, admissions of guilt that reeked of reluctance, and a sense of betrayal so profound it could fill the Thames. We had placed our trust in these men, expecting them to steer us through the pandemic's treacherous waters. Instead, we were handed a masterclass in chaos, a cohort of leaders so entwined in their own turmoil, they couldn't see the cliff edge until they were already over it.

Unearthing the Hidden Truths

As we navigate through the wreckage of this governmental disaster, we're confronted with a glaring, infuriating truth: key pieces of the puzzle are missing. WhatsApp messages from none other than Boris Johnson himself have vanished into thin air for a crucial period, leaving us with gaping holes in our understanding of the government's actions during our darkest hours.

And it's not just Boris. Sunak, our current Prime Minister, sits in the same precarious boat, having "misplaced" messages from a vital period as well. It's a convenient amnesia, isn't it? Vital exchanges, crucial for piecing together the full extent of the government's disarray, are now just echoes in the wind.

The context here is monumental. These missing messages aren't just digital footprints; they're the keys to understanding the depths of the betrayal we faced. We needed trust and transparency, and instead, we got evasion and erasure. This isn't just incompetence; it's a fucking mockery of accountability.

And amidst this digital black hole, the WhatsApp revelations we do have lay bare a government in crisis. Simon Case, with his digital outbursts and moments of desperation, has thrown us a lifeline to the truth. But it's not enough. We need the whole picture, not just fragmented glimpses of the chaos.

The government has failed us, spectacularly and unabashedly. And now, as we demand accountability, we also demand transparency. We need to unearth these hidden truths, to expose the full extent of the disarray and hold those responsible to account.

We need leaders who understand the gravity of their actions, who respect the trust placed in them by the nation. We need humility, not arrogance. We need responsibility, not evasion. The road ahead is treacherous, filled with the debris of broken trust and failed leadership.

But if there's one thing this inquiry has illuminated, it's that we cannot, and we will not, let this be the end of the story. The government's dirty laundry is out in the open, and we demand a fucking cleaning crew.

So here's the message, loud and clear, to those at the top: You've bollocksed up. You've betrayed the nation, and it's high time you face the music. Find those messages, come clean, and for once in your political lives, do the right thing.

The nation is watching, our patience worn thin. We demand accountability, we demand transparency, and we will accept nothing less. Our trust is shattered, but our resolve is unbreakable. Fix this mess, or get the hell out.

Rising from the Ashes of Deceit

So here we are, at the bitter end of this tumultuous

journey through the underbelly of governmental incompetence and deceit. We've waded through the swamp of WhatsApp messages, witnessed the disgraceful display of evasion and arrogance, and now, it's time to rise.

This isn't just a call for accountability; it's a fucking war cry for change.

The inquiry has laid the sins of the government bare for all to see, but this is not where our story ends. It's where it begins. We've seen the rot, we've smelled the stench of corruption, and now, we must cleanse the wound, no matter how deep the cut.

The missing WhatsApp messages, the convenient gaps in communication from Boris and Sunak, they're not just oversights; they're glaring red flags, screaming for attention. We need those messages, not tomorrow, not when it suits them, but now. We need the full, unadulterated truth, and we will accept nothing less.

Our trust has been betrayed, our faith shattered, but our spirit remains unbroken. We, the people, have a voice, and it's time to fucking use it. We demand transparency, we demand accountability, and we demand a government that's worthy of our trust.

So rise up, my friends, and let your voices be heard. Write to your MPs, take to the streets, do whatever it takes to hold these bastards to account. They've played us for fools, but we are not their pawns. We are the people, and we will not be silenced.

The road ahead is long and fraught with obstacles, but we've faced worse, and we've come out stronger. It's time to reclaim our power, to restore trust in our government, and to build a future that's free from the shackles of deceit and incompetence.

We deserve better. We demand better. And by God, we will get better.

RAINBOW RUCKUS: THE QUEER QUANDARY AND OUR TECHNICOLOR TUSSLES

Dive into the dazzling debacle of "queer," where every shade of the spectrum clashes, converges, and carouses in a boisterous brawl for identity and unity.

Alright, people, let's cut the crap and dive into one hell of a queer tale - and I mean that in every sense of the word. "Queer" isn't just a word; it's a suitcase packed with bombshells and glitter, a Pandora's box that's been through the wringer and back. We've snatched it from the jaws of haters, scrubbed off the spit, and pinned it to our chests like a medal of hard-won honour and dignity.

But now? Now we're in a bit of a pickle, a real shitshow within our own queer kingdom. This isn't just about a word; it's about who we are, where we've been, and where the hell we're headed. It's about the "queer" we parade on banners, the one we debate over espresso shots or whiskey sours, and the one some people want to chuck in the trash.

So, saddle up your best show pony, my queer brethren (and sisteren?), and curious allies. We're about to zigzag through the good, the bad, and the downright ugly of "queer." From its first innocent breaths to its years as a slur that could cut you deeper than a drag queen's side-eye, to its badass rebirth in the fiery furnaces of LGBTQ+ defiance.

We'll navigate the shitstorm it's stirred up lately, with the LGB Alliance and others throwing punches like it's the last round before closing time. It's messy, it's heated, and it's got more drama than a reality TV reunion.

But this isn’t just another queer telenovela. This is our story, our word, and our future. So, let's get to the nitty-gritty, the heart and soul of "queer," and see if we can't find some common ground - or at least agree to disagree with a flick of fabulousness.

Toast to the word that's been through hell and back, just like us. Here's to "queer," darlings - let's give it the spotlight it deserves.

Queer's Quirky Quest: From Odd to Outcast

First things first, let's time-travel back to when "queer" was just a twinkle in the English language's eye, way before it got drafted into the cultural wars. Picture this: it's the 16th century, and "queer" is just chilling with a meaning that wouldn't raise a single eyebrow today. It meant “odd,” “peculiar,” or “out of the ordinary” - like your Uncle Gary’s obsession with collecting creepy clowns or that neighbour who builds UFOs in his back garden.

Back then, calling something "queer" was like saying, "Oh, that's kinda funky," not "I hate your guts." It was the word you'd use for the eccentric hat you bought at the Renaissance fair, not for a person you wanted to throw rotten tomatoes at.

But fast-forward a couple of hundred years, and "queer" starts to pick up some serious baggage. By the late 19th and early 20th centuries, this little word had wandered down the back alleys of society and gotten itself a bad rep. Suddenly, "queer" wasn't just quirky; it was a full-blown insult, a slap across the face to anyone who didn't fit the straight-laced (pun intended) norms of the time.

You see, society back then was about as flexible as a two-by-four, and anything that didn't line up with the "man marries woman, has 2.5 kids, and a picket fence" dream was branded as wrong, deviant, "queer." And so, a word that once danced around the edges of oddness was now being used to ostracize and oppress.

It's a classic case of a good word gone bad, like when your favourite song gets overplayed until you want to scream, or when a delicious cake falls victim to a nasty food fight. "Queer" got dragged through the mud, tarred, and feathered, and turned into a verbal weapon. And damn, did it sting.

So, there you have it - the rocky road "queer" travelled, from a harmless descriptor of the strange and unusual to a barbed term that could slice through a person's dignity. Stay tuned, though, because this word's about to flip the script and become a battle cry for a whole new era.

The Dark Ages of "Queer": From Slur to Stigma

Fast forward to our more recent history and we've landed smack dab in the gutter years of "queer," when the word was about as welcome as a fart in an elevator. It's the dark ages for this once-innocent term, and society's wielding it like a blunt instrument to bash anything that dares to defy the norm.

This was the era when "queer" went from being a verbal side-eye to a full-on snarl, a way to mark someone as 'other,' as less-than. It was a label slapped on people who loved differently, who defied the cookie-cutter blueprint of sexuality and gender that was considered as sacred as Sunday roast.

You've got to understand the backdrop here: we're talking about times when the mere suggestion of being gay could land you in the slammer or worse. It was an era of witch-hunts against anyone who didn't march in the straight (and narrow) parade – a time of police raids on bars, of names shamefully whispered, of lives lived in the shadows. "Queer" became a weapon of fear and control, a way to keep the “unruly” in check.

The social and cultural scene wasn't doing anyone any favours, either. Religion was thumping its chest like a gorilla, decreeing what was natural and what was an abomination. The law was a lapdog to these beliefs, all too eager to bite. And let's not even start on the media, which was painting "queer" people as deviants, as bogeymen lurking in dark alleys, waiting to corrupt the innocent.

In the hands of the ignorant and the intolerant, "queer" was a slur that cut deeper than a knife, a stark reminder that you were the outcast, the one society could do without. It was a way to alienate and vilify, to turn a person's identity into a punchline or a horror story.

But even the darkest night breaks into dawn, and "queer" was about to be snatched from the jaws of bigotry and polished back into something fierce, shiny, and proud. The pejorative years were a crucible, and from that fire, a fabulous phoenix was ready to rise. Keep your eyes peeled, people, because the comeback kid's about to enter the stage.

Snatching "Queer" Back: A Badge of Honour

Alright, buckle up, buttercups, because we're diving into the badass chapter of our "queer" saga. This is where the LGBTQ+ gang flips the script, grabs "queer" by the scruff, and says, “You're with us now, bitch.”

The reclamation of "queer" didn't happen overnight. It was a Herculean effort, like trying to turn a Wetherspoons into an Abba themed disco after last call. But damn, the determination was there. Activists and outcasts, the marginalized and the maligned, they all came together with a collective middle finger raised to the establishment.

Picture it: the AIDS crisis is raging, and the government's about as helpful as tits on a sofa. It's a time of pain, of anger, of heart-breaking loss - but also of fierce solidarity. The word "queer" started cropping up, not whispered in fear, but chanted in the streets. It became a rallying cry, a call to arms against a society that seemed hell-bent on ignoring their plight.

Enter stage left groups like Queer Nation, badass warriors of the word, who snatched "queer" out of the toxic sludge and wore it like a crown. They were loud, proud, and unapologetically in-your-face. "We're here, we're queer, get used to it!" they roared, and the streets echoed with the sound of a community taking back its power.

And it wasn't just about being loud; it was about being seen. Pride parades turned "queer" into a banner that fluttered in every colour of the rainbow. Art and literature embraced it, with writers and poets weaving it into works that bled truth and beauty. "Queer" became synonymous with defiance, with the refusal to be invisible or silent.

Icons popped up like daisies in this reclaimed field. Sylvia Rivera, Marsha P. Johnson - names that stood for the gritty, gutsy fight to be recognized as human, as deserving of love and respect. They didn't just use "queer"; they infused it with their spirit, their fight, their unyielding hope.

This reclamation was a revolution in itself, a transformative spell that turned a slur into a symbol of pride. "Queer" became a badge of honour, a testament to survival and strength. It was a word that encapsulated the diversity of a community that refused to be defined by anyone else's terms.

So, chapeau to those trailblazers who took a word steeped in hate and cast it in gold. Because of them, "queer" isn't just a word; it's a legacy, a story of a journey from the shadows into the blazing light of day.

Queer Today – A Community Divided

Fast forward to today, and "queer" is sitting pretty at the cool kids' table, sipping a craft beer, and shooting the breeze about intersectionality. But hold up—there's trouble brewing in paradise. The word that once united us is now a bit of a troublemaker, stirring the pot like it's cooking up a storm of contention.

You've got the old guard and the new bloods, each with their own take on "queer." For some, it's a cosy blanket, all-inclusive and warm. For others, it's got more edges than a porcupine at a punk rock concert, too spiky to hold without getting pricked.

Now, here's where the plot thickens, and the shit hits the fan. There's a schism, a crack in the LGBTQ + family portrait, right between the L's, G's, B's, and the T's and Q's. Some people are hell-bent on turning "queer" into a battleground, a line in the sand that says, "Cross this and you're not one of us." As if we haven't got enough on our plates fighting the good fight, now we've got friendly fire?

And let's talk about those LGB Alliance types,

sharpening their knives on the grindstone of "traditional values." They're slicing the word "queer" out of the acronym like a surgeon with the shakes, claiming it's gone too far from its roots, that it's become a catch-all that's catching too much. They're pushing for a divide, harking back to a "simpler" time. But let's call a spade a spade – there is nothing simple about stripping away someone's identity.

It's a bit of a clusterfuck, isn’t it? On one hand, "queer" is this beautiful, reclaimed badge of honour. On the other, it's a word that’s being wielded like a club in a bar brawl, causing rifts in the very community it helped to build. We're standing in the middle of a linguistic tug-of-war, and the rope’s starting to fray.

We've come a long way, but it's a kick in the teeth to see "queer" become a tool for infighting. We used to be a glorious human jigsaw puzzle; now it feels like someone's trying to jam the pieces together with a hammer. The word that was supposed to be our shield is being used to throw shade, and that, my friends, is a bitter pill to swallow.

What the hell happened to the "all for one and one for all" spirit? It’s like watching your favourite band break up over creative differences. We're all on the same stage, but it seems like we're reading from different scripts. "Queer" is our word, damn it - it's supposed to bring us together, not tear us apart.

So here we stand, at the crossroads, with "queer" as our compass. Question is, which way do we go? Do we let it divide us, or do we remember the battles fought, the tears shed, and the lives lost that gave it power? It's high time we figured it out because there's a storm coming, and we need all hands-on deck.

The Role of Language in Identity and Inclusivity

So, let's talk turkey about something that's as clear as day, but often gets lost in the hullabaloo: Language is more than a collection of sounds and symbols. It's the framework of our identities, the architect of our communities, and for the LGBTQ+ tribe, it's the vibrant thread that's woven into the very essence of who we are.

"Queer" has played the part of a linguistic chameleon, a word that's danced through the ages, reflecting our struggles, triumphs, and the rich tapestry of our collective being. It's been a raised fist in the air of defiance, a subtle nod of acknowledgment in the face of adversity. But let's not forget, the magic of a word is bound up in its intent.

Words evolve, they kick against the pricks, they change their spots and sometimes their entire bloody wardrobe. That's their magic. But they're also like a Swiss Army knife - they can patch things up or cut deep, all hinged on who's holding it and why. "Queer" has been a soothing balm and a bitter pill, a marker of pride and, at times, a brand of suffering.

And here's the real meat of it: context is king. Murmur "queer" with affection, and it's a hearth-fire on a cold night. Hurl it with scorn, and it's a slap across the face. It's adaptable, that's for sure. It's all about the who, the where, the how. The same word that kindles pride can also ostracize, all because of the energy it rides in on.

Inclusivity? That's the goal, the dream, the prize. But when "queer" is flung around like a hot potato in the back-and-forth of social media spats, we sometimes lose sight of the fact that we're all on the same side. Language is our toolbox, and we've got to use it to construct connections, not chasms. We have to ensure it's a key, not a lock.

Language, the slippery creature that it is, can be as hard to pin down as a shadow. But here's the clincher - we're at the helm. We can direct it towards new horizons or down into the abyss. It’s up to us to shape it, to tailor it, and to make sure it wraps around everyone in this gloriously diverse clan we call the LGBTQ+ community.

Within the grand quilt of queerness, each strand, each hue, has its rightful spot. "Queer" can be the strand that fortifies the fabric or the one that tugs it loose. We must be deliberate, savvy, and ensure that when we wield "queer," it throws open gates, not slams them. It's high time we band together and harness the true potential of words - the power to bind us, to raise us up, to make us indomitable. And isn't that the whole point?

Moving Forward – Reflection and Unity

For anyone who is still reading, let's put our cards on the table, shall we? The road's been bumpy, the night's been long, and we've all got our share of bruises. But as dawn breaks over the horizon, it's time to think about how we, the grand old LGBTQ+ family, can step up our game. It's about finding the glue to stick us together when the going gets tough - because let's face it, it often does, and I sadly feel that we have yet another rough few years ahead of us.

Linguistic squabbles, ideological tiffs, they're like family spats - they sting because the bonds are so damn tight. But here's the kicker: it's precisely because we give a damn. We care about our history, our present, and the legacy we're leaving for the bright-eyed youngsters snapping at our heels. Our collective history is a mosaic of struggles and victories, a colourful tale of tenacity that can't be ignored.

Now, as for "queer" and the ruckus it's kicked up, it's time to take a breather. To remember that words have power because we breathe life into them. They're not set in stone; they're as alive as you and me, changing and growing with every heartbeat of our community. It's time to harness that power, to use it to build bridges, not barriers.

Unity doesn't mean we all sing the same tune or step to the same beat. No, it's about harmonizing our diverse voices, about strutting our varied and fabulous dances in a way that makes the whole club pulse with life. It's about finding the common beat that unites us, the shared pulse of humanity that makes us stronger together.

Reflecting on our shared journey, let's embrace the word "queer" not as a shackle but as a symbol of our adaptability and strength. Let's celebrate the rebels, the trailblazers, the quiet warriors who've carried that word like a torch through the darkest of nights. It's a badge of honour, a whisper of the past, and a shout for the future.

As we look ahead, let's pledge to tackle the divides with the same courage and spirit that have marked our past battles. Let's promise to listen more, to extend a hand even when it's hard, and to remember that in the grand scheme of things, we're all part of something much bigger than ourselves.

So, to the LGBTQ+ family, here's to moving forward with eyes wide open, hearts on our sleeves, and "queer" firmly in our grasp - not as a weapon, but as a tool of enlightenment and unity. Let's march into tomorrow with the full, dazzling spectrum of our community in tow, turning our faces to the sun and stepping out, together, into a future where every one of us is valued, celebrated, and, above all, loved.

The Journey of "Queer" and the Path Ahead

So, what a fucking rollercoaster it's been, huh?

From its innocent beginnings to the slings and arrows of outrageous fortune, to a banner under which we've rallied, "queer" has been through the wringer. It's been slurred, sanctified, celebrated, and scorned, but damn it, it's ours. It's a word that's as multifaceted as the community it represents, a community as varied as the stars in the sky or the fish in the sea.

Let's not kid ourselves; the journey's been tough. Words can be double-edged swords, and "queer" has been both a wound and a balm. But it's also been a source of power, a rallying cry for those of us who defy the norm, who colour outside the lines, who live and love with a fierce intensity that knows no bounds.

In this wild garden of humanity, inclusivity is the water that lets the flowers bloom. It's what allows us to bask in the kaleidoscope of experiences that make up the LGBTQ+ community. Understanding is the sunlight that nourishes our growth, helping us to see each other not as threats, but as companions on this journey.

And solidarity? Well, it's the soil that grounds us, rich with the nutrients of our shared history, our collective pain, and our combined joy. It's what keeps us rooted when the storms hit, reminding us that we've weathered worse, and we'll damn well weather whatever comes next.

Personally, I'm clinging to the hope that "queer" can be a term of unity, not division - a word that encapsulates the wild, wondrous spectrum of who we are and who we can be. It's a term that should be worn with pride, a testament to how far we've come and a beacon for the road ahead.

So, let's lock arms, my queer comrades, and march forward with heads held high. Let's remember that our strength lies in our togetherness, in the shared beats of our hearts, and in the collective roar of our voices. Let's be the fucking magnificent rainbow of change we wish to see in the world, united by our past, our present, and the future we'll forge together.

Here's to "queer," in all its glory - may it continue to light our way and remind us that, in this vast and often confusing world, we have each other. And that, my friends, is worth its weight in gold.

FLUSHING FUTURE: THE UK'S WATER WOES AND THE TORRENT OF INCOMPETENCE AT THE HELM

Dive into the murky waters of mismanagement and neglect as we unravel the effluent saga of environmental disregard, led by none other than Therese "Nellie the Effluent" Coffey.

Brace yourselves and grab a hold of your nostrils, my dear friends, because today we're diving headfirst into a cesspit of monumental bullshit (and not necessarily figuratively either), courtesy of none other than the UK's Environment Secretary, the recently renamed Therese "Nellie the Effluent" Coffey.

A Symphony of Shit: The Water Crisis Obfuscated

When asked about the state of the water systems in our fair land, our dearest Nellie had the absolute audacity to spew forth such a torrent of claptrap that even a seasoned bullshit detector like me was left gobsmacked, unable to find the right words and was left with a brief, punchy but not very descriptive *"What. The. Actual. Fuck."*

That was all I could muster when I first heard her claim that we have the "best drinking water in the world" and that our beaches have been practically sparkling since 2010. Is she taking the actual piss? Or is she living in a parallel universe where raw sewage in our rivers is the latest health craze? I actually had to compose myself for a full day to make sure that I wasn't hallucinating after being exposed to that clip!

So, let's slice through the bullshit and lay down some cold, hard facts, shall we? Thames Water, that pinnacle of corporate fuckery, is drowning in a £14 billion debt cesspool, while brazenly spewing sewage into our rivers with the kind of abandon that would make a drunkard blush. And it's not just them; the whole damn industry is a shambolic parade of incompetence and greed.

Over 300,000 sewage spills last year, and leakage enough to fill more than 1,200 Olympic-sized swimming pools every goddamn day. And what are we, the hard-paying public, getting in return? Jack shit, that's what. Bills are through the roof, and set to climb even higher, while the water companies laugh all the way to the bank, dividends in one hand and a shiny turd in the other. And OfWat, you ask? Those supposed guardians of our waterways? About as useful as tits on a fish, letting these water barons run amok while our rivers turn to toxic sludge.

Nellie's Notorious Negligence

Let's go back to Nellie for a brief moment, because his isn't her first rodeo of incompetence. Since being elected in 2010, she has consistently shown a callous, mean disregard for the public's well-being with a gay abandon that is staggering. She voted against same-sex marriage and supported the sale of our public forests.

Let's also not forget her dazzling performance as Pensions Secretary, where she seemed to have taken a masterclass in the art of sweeping shit under the rug. Oh, it was a sight to behold, folks! Reports? What reports? Damning evidence of mismanagement and foul play? Never heard of them! She sat on those reports like a hen on her eggs, guarding them with her life while the rest of us were left in the dark, wondering what fresh hell was being concocted in the depths of her department.

It's like she's got a PhD in Procrastination and a master's in Misdirection. And now, she's brought her unique brand of bureaucratic bullshit to the Environment Department, where she seems to be on a one-woman mission to take us back to the dark ages, one sewage spill at a time. But hey, at least she's consistent, right? Consistently terrible, that is.

This water scandal though? This is her pièce de résistance of failure most foul. Under her watch, we've got a full-blown, omnishambolic water crisis on our hands, and she's there, grinning like an absolute moron, telling us everything is hunky-fucking-dory.

So here we are, paying through the nose for water, while our rivers turn into open sewers and our beaches look like open-air lavatories. But sure, Nellie, everything is just peachy. We've got the best drinking water in the world, haven't we? And our beaches? Well, they're just a paradise of cleanliness.

This is a clusterfuck of epic proportions, and it's happening on your watch. You can spew all the lies you wants on national television, but the stench of this scandal is so overpowering that not even your special brand of bullshit can mask it.

A Blight on Public Health: Sewage Spills and 19th Century Horrors

Now, let's talk about the very real and very disgusting health risks associated with these sewage spills. You know, the kind of risks that can lead to serious illness and disease? Yeah, those risks.

We're talking about exposure to harmful bacteria, viruses, and parasites that thrive in sewage-contaminated waters. Think E. coli, salmonella, and hepatitis A. These are not your run-of-the-mill tummy bugs which you pass in a few days; they are serious, life-threatening diseases that can cause severe gastrointestinal illness, liver failure, permanent disability and even death.

And the really scary part? This isn't the first time we've seen this kind of public health crisis. Cast your minds back to the 19th Century, a time of workhouses, Jack The Ripper, regular episodes of cholera outbreaks and filthy living conditions. A time when sewage ran freely in the streets and people died by the thousands from waterborne diseases. It took a revolution in public sanitation to bring an end to the horror and save countless lives.

But now, here we are in the 21st Century, and it seems like the Tories are hell-bent on taking us back in time as quickly as possible. Under Nellie the Effluent's watch, our rivers and beaches are becoming open sewers, and the risk of waterborne disease is becoming all too real.

The Time for Action is Now

So, what do we do about it? Are we going to sit back and let "Nellie the Effluent" and her band of merry shitgibbons turn our once-great nation into a literal cesspool? Hell no. It's time to raise hell and demand accountability.

Let's not just stand here and drown in this river of governmental incompetence and corporate greed. It's high time we put on our metaphorical waders and start shovelling the shit out of the system. First things first, we need to boot Nellie the Effluent out of her ivory tower and replace her with someone who actually gives a damn about our environment. Someone who won't just spew bullshit and call it potpourri.

Next, let's put these water companies on a tight leash, shall we? Fine them into oblivion for every drop of sewage they dare spill into our rivers and seas. And OfWat? It's time to grow a pair and actually do your job. No more pussyfooting around; hold these water barons accountable for their environmental atrocities.

And us? We, the pissed-off public, need to raise hell and make our voices heard. Write to your MPs, protest, shout from the rooftops if you have to. Let's turn this effluent tide and reclaim our rivers, beaches, and dignity.

We've had enough of living in a Dickensian nightmare; it's time to drag our country, kicking and screaming, if necessary, back into the 21st century.

FROM KAFKAESQUE ORDEALS TO BRAVERMAN'S BIG TOP: A MIGRANT'S BATTLE CRY FOR BRITISH HUMANITY

Join the crusade against the Home Office's absurdities and the callous crackdown on compassion in the UK's latest migrant saga

Pull up a chair, pour yourself a steaming mug of your favourite brew, and let's have a chinwag. You're not just another anonymous click to me; you're the reason I hammer away at this keyboard, spilling my guts and sharing the kind of tales that would make your nan's hair curl.

Back in 2016, I packed my life into two suitcases and, with a heart full of hope, set foot on this green and sometimes pleasant land. I dreamt of a grand adventure in the UK, a nation famed for its underdog victories and "keep calm and carry on" spirit. But instead, I found myself caught in the remnants of a system still reeling from the Windrush scandal – a system that couldn't find humanity if it was printed on their passport.

I've been through the wringer – from the comical to the downright Kafkaesque. I've paid through the nose for the privilege of proving I can speak the Queen's English to someone whose grasp of the language was, let's just say, not quite up to par. It's these experiences that give me the fire to share the unvarnished truth about the Hostile Environment – a policy as welcoming as a hedgehog in a sleeping bag.

So, let's tread this path together. I promise it'll

be more than a mere rant. It's a saga of the extraordinary resilience in the face of policies that would make less stoic souls crumble. And it's a call to arms, because if I've learnt anything, it's that silence is the best friend of injustice. So, let's make some noise.

Now, on with the show.

Navigating the Home Office's Bloody Maze

Welcome to my world – a world where the phrase "Hostile Environment" is less about the weather and more about a Home Office policy that seems to take a perverse pleasure in turning life into an obstacle course for migrants. It's as if someone took the rulebook for decency, chucked it into the Thames, and said, "There, now navigate that, you lot."

Take the English language test, for instance. Handing over £150 felt like a donation to the "Help Confuse a Migrant" fund, especially when the test conductor struggled more with English than I did. It's like buying a ticket to a comedy show, only the joke's on you, and the punchline is a kick in the teeth.

But wait, there's more. The whole process of staying in this country is a theatre of the absurd. You must prove your marriage is real over and over again, as if you're renewing your vows but to a crowd of sceptical bureaucrats instead of loved ones. You offer up years of text messages and photos, intimate moments served up for inspection, just to get a stamp of approval.

Let's talk about finding a home. Trying to rent a flat with a visa is like bringing a tofu steak to a barbecue – you're not going to be the most popular person there. The moment landlords hear "visa", you can almost hear the clunk of the door slamming shut in your face. It's a wonder I've ever managed to find a roof over my head that wasn't made of soggy cardboard.

And employment? Jesus, Mary, and Joseph, it's a hoot. My qualifications might as well be written on cocktail napkins for all the good they do me once HR hears the word "visa". It's like you're some sort of extra-terrestrial being asking for a job, not a living, breathing professional.

I would like to stress, I am one of the "lucky" ones – my English is on point, I had some savings to cushion the blows, and my skin doesn't scare the easily spooked. Yet, I've been given the cold shoulder more times than I care to count, just because my right to be here is stapled into a passport rather than birthed on soil. Spare a thought for those who don't have the same cards to play with.

So here we are, living out our very own British farce, complete with a government that seems to believe making life hell for migrants is a jolly good pastime. But don't worry, it's all just a day in the life of the UK's immigration obstacle course – designed by those who wouldn't know compassion if it came with instructions.

The Outrageous Odyssey Continues: Braverman's Tent Tantrum

Now, let's wade deeper into the murky waters of the Home Office, where compassion is as rare as a sunny British summer. The latest act in this ongoing drama stars our Home Secretary, Cruella Braverman, who seems hell-bent on turning heartlessness into government policy.

Braverman's latest brainwave is to outlaw tents for the homeless, making the very act of offering a temporary shelter to those in dire need a finable offence. It's as if she's trying to outdo the Grinch, only instead of stealing Christmas, she's snatching away the last shreds of dignity from those struggling to survive. It's not just cruel; it's a policy that would make Dickens himself scribble furiously in his grave.

This isn't about cleaning up the streets or solving homelessness; it's about pushing the problem out of sight, pretending that if we can't see it, it doesn't exist. It's about criminalising the very essence of charity. Imagine being fined for offering a coat to someone in the cold - that's the level of absurdity we've reached.

And let's not forget about the Rwanda scheme, a plan so outlandish and inhumane that it feels plucked from the pages of a dystopian novel. Sending asylum seekers thousands of miles away to a country with its own complex issues is not just irresponsible; it's a complete abdication of Britain's duty to those seeking refuge. It's a policy that looks at international norms and human rights and laughs in the face of both.

All this, mind you, while our dear Cruella stands on the shoulders of giants, claiming to uphold British values. If British values involve treating the vulnerable as a nuisance to be exported or swept under the carpet, then we must ask ourselves: what have we become?

But here's the rub: this isn't the end of the story. It's a call to arms, a rallying cry for those of us who still believe in a Britain that cares, that extends a helping hand rather than clenching a fist. It's time for us to stand up and say, "Not in my name."

Now, keep in mind, this journey isn't over. It's just getting started, and we're going to take this whirlwind of indignation and turn it into a force for change. We won't stand idly by while the Home Office morphs into an institution that would make Kafka blush.

Rousing the Ranks of the Righteous

So here we are, my band of beleaguered brothers, sisters, and non-binary resistors, at the precipice of a battle for the soul of this sceptred isle. It's time to transform our seething rage into a clarion call that echoes through the hallowed halls of the Home Office and beyond.

We've been witnesses to a cruel charade, where the vulnerable are vilified and the destitute are demonised. But this narrative is ours to rewrite. We must seize the pen from those who would draft a future filled with fear and exclusion, and author a new chapter of hope and inclusion.

The tent debacle is a perfect metaphor for the short-sightedness of the current regime. To criminalise the offering of shelter is to punish empathy, to fine compassion. It's a policy born not of a desire to solve the problem of homelessness, but to erase it from the public eye, to render the afflicted invisible rather than to alleviate their suffering.

Our response must be as loud as it is clear: We are a nation of more than mere merchants of cold commerce; we are a community that thrives on warmth and generosity. We must not let our legacy be stained by the ink of heartless statutes.

To those ensnared by the Home Office's Kafkaesque maze, I say: Your voices are heard. Your struggles are seen. And to the architects of these ordeals, I say: We are not mere pawns in your game of callous calculus. We are the lifeblood of this nation, the tapestry of its future, and we refuse to be snipped away to suit your narrative.

It's high time we rally, not just with tweets and hashtags, but with boots on the ground, with pens in hand, and votes at the ready. We must support the charities that face fines for their acts of kindness and back the politicians who dare to stand against the tide of tyranny.

Let's not be content with being the generation that merely raged against the dying of the light. Let's be the generation that rekindled the flame of justice and humanity. We must demand reparations for those wronged by hostile policies and ensure safeguards are erected to prevent such misdeeds from recurring.

To the would-be despots, the Cruellas in high offices, we declare: You may have the stage, but we are the chorus, and our song is one of unyielding resistance. We will not be muted. We will not be side-lined. We are the beating heart of this nation, and we will be heard.

Stand with me, with us, as we fight not for a Britain of fear and fences, but for one of open arms and open hearts. Let's make our stand here and now, for a Home Office that offers a hearth for the weary traveller and a chance for every soul to find a home.

So, who's with me? Who's ready to transform this justified anger into a campaign for compassion? It's about bloody time we steer this ship away from the rocks of ruin and towards the safe harbours of humanity and hope.

Together, let's show that the spirit of Britain isn't defined by the narrowness of its borders but by the boundless capacity of its compassion. Let's not just make a stand; let's make a difference. For in the end, it is not the vitriol of our words that will be remembered, but the virtue of our actions.

JAB JESTERS: THE WACKY WORLD OF VACCINE MISINFORMATIO N

Join me on a rollicking ride through history's most "viral" myths, from snake oil to Twitter threads – no tin foil hats required!

Well, strap in and slap on your sceptic's hat, because we're about to embark on a whimsical whack-a-mole adventure through the wild world of vaccine misinformation. Remember when the craziest thing you heard all day was that gummy bears were part of a balanced diet or that tequila counted as a serving of agave? Those were simpler times, my friends.

Our journey today? We're diving headfirst into the delightful dumpster fire that is the anti-vax movement, a place where logic goes to die, and science is about as welcome as a porcupine in a sleeping bag. You've seen the memes; you've dodged the Facebook rants, and hell, maybe you've even had a run-in with Aunt Karen at the family BBQ, where she tried to convince you that the COVID-19 vaccine is just Big Pharma's way of turning you into a walking, talking 5G antenna.

So, after much ado - and because frankly, I love a good shitshow - I've decided to don my hazmat suit and wade deeper into the cesspool of pseudo-science. We'll chuckle, we'll cringe, and we might just facepalm so hard we leave a mark. But fear not! We'll navigate this quagmire with the finesse of a cat avoiding a puddle.

Because if we're going to tackle this beast, we might as well have a laugh while we're at it. After all, if you can't find humour in the absolute circus that is vaccine misinformation, you're probably not paying attention. So, let's raise a glass (or a syringe if you're feeling thematic) to the journey ahead. It's going to be one hell of a ride.

Cowpox To Conspiracy: A Hilarious History Of Hypodermic Hysteria

Alright, I hope you're comfortable and well settled, because it's time to take a time machine (not a DeLorean, unfortunately only in our imagination for today) back to the days when medicine was as much about magic as it was about science. Our destination? The bizarre bazaar of vaccine misinformation, a place where facts are optional, and fear is the currency.

First stop, the 1790s. Picture this: Edward Jenner, a man with a dream and a dairy maid's cowpox sore. Fast forward, and poof! Smallpox vaccination is born. But not everyone's popping champagne. Oh no. Instead, there's talk that if you get the jab, you might start mooing on a full moon. That's right, folks were terrified they'd sprout cow parts. No bull!

Now, scoot over to the 19th century, when vaccines are all the rage - like frock coats and typhoid. But the anti-vax sentiment is festering like a bad case of the mumps. Pamphlets spread like wildfire, claiming vaccines are more nefarious than a moustache-twirling villain tying a damsel to the train tracks.

Enter the 20th century, when we've swapped horse-drawn carriages for Ford Model Ts, but some folks still think vaccines are the devil's brew. The polio vaccine? Why, it's nothing but a government ploy to - I don't know - make you dance the Charleston uncontrollably? The details were fuzzy, but the fear? Crystal clear.

And how can we forget the 1990s? The decade of Tamagotchis and Titanic, and one discredited study linking vaccines to autism that spread faster than a Spice Girls hit. Never mind that it's been debunked harder than the idea of a flat Earth - this little nugget of nonsense still gets trotted out like it's gospel by the Church of the Eternal Side-Eye.

Let's not overlook the more exotic flavours of vaccine paranoia: the belief that a shot could turn you into a magnet (fridge ornaments, beware!), or the classic, "It'll alter your DNA!" Because apparently, some think a needle prick can turn you into Spider-Man. If only.

So here we are, in the 21st century, where we can 3D print a pizza but still can't convince some people that vaccines won't make them grow a third eyeball. The landscape of vaccine misinformation is as wild and woolly as ever, a testament to human creativity if not intelligence. And the moral of the story? Fear is infectious, but luckily, laughter is the best medicine.

Likes, Lies, And Viral Lunacy: The Social Media Misinformation Pandemic

Moving on, I'm happy to shout "Step right Up", because our next stop is to head to the digital carnival, where the information is fast, the facts are loose, and everyone's two cents are thrown into the ring with the grace of a plastic chair being blown around in a windstorm. Welcome to the age of social media, where misinformation goes viral faster than a celebrity nip slip, and the truth is playing catch-up like it's on a pair of crutches.

Here, algorithms are the puppet masters, and they love a good conspiracy theory like a cat loves catnip. They say, "You enjoyed that video about flat earth? Here's one about vaccines turning your blood into a 5G hotspot!" And just like that, you're down the rabbit hole, where up is down, left is right, and science is just an opinion.

Social media has turned every Tom, Dick, and Harriet with a Wi-Fi connection into an armchair expert. Gone are the days of soapbox rants at the town square, where the audience was limited to a few pigeons and a guy named Dave. Now, Dave's online, and he's got a following because he "speaks the truth" and has flashy graphics to prove it.

We've traded the snake oil salesman for the influencer who peddles pseudoscience with the perfect filter. Forget the peer-reviewed studies; we're living in an era where a well-curated Instagram feed is all the credentials you need to become a health guru.

Echo chambers? They're not just for acoustics

anymore. They're virtual rooms where the only sound is the reverberating clap of a thousand people who just love that you agree with them. Here, the silliest claims get amplified in a feedback loop, like a game of telephone where the message starts as "vaccines save lives" and ends up as "vaccines are mind control for the lizard people in charge."

And let's have a round of applause for the armchair warriors, who share links like they're throwing grenades over the trenches. "Take that, Big Pharma!" they cry, posting an article from a site that also claims Elvis is alive and living on Mars.

In this grand stage of digital delirium, whispers turn into roars with the click of a button. The town crier's bell has been replaced by the notification ding, and the soapbox has given way to the global megaphone of social media, where you don't have to be right - you just have to be the loudest shouter.

So, what's the net effect? A perfect storm of panic and paranoia, where the truth doesn't just get stretched; it gets a full-on facelift. And in the middle of this storm, common sense is the umbrella that everyone forgets at home.

The Rogues' Gallery Of Misinformation Maestros

Now, let's move on to the next section of our tour through the not so true, the grand circus of vaccine misinformation, where the clowns often forget their makeup but never their ability to juggle facts with fiction. In this corner of the tent, we showcase a flamboyant parade of misinformed maestros, each vying for the title of "Most Viral Virtuoso" in the echo chamber orchestra.

First up, we've got the "Wellness Guru," whose only credential is a radiant complexion and an Instagram feed that's more filtered than a conspiracy theorist's truth. They peddle a heady mix of ancient remedies and modern mumbo-jumbo, convincing you that a shot of wheatgrass can somehow outmuscle modern medicine. Their mantra? "Big Pharma is out to get you, but my £99 detox tea will save your soul."

Next, the "Armchair Epidemiologist" leaps into the fray. By day, they're just your average Joe, but by night they transform into a one-person think tank, armed with YouTube clips and a subscription to "Conspiracies-R-Us." They'll cite studies from the prestigious University of I-Read-It-On-The-Internet, where peer review means getting a like from their buddy Dave.

Let's not overlook the "Rebranded Quack," a creature of mythical contradictions. They've taken an oath to do no harm, yet their Instagram is a smorgasbord of anti-vax appetizers. They throw around terms like "toxin" and "natural immunity" with the same gusto they reserve for cashing in on their line of immunity-boosting sneakers.

Hovering in the shadows is the "Political Pundit," who sees viruses not as a public health issue but as a political football to be punted across rallies. They're the type who thinks wearing a mask infringes on their freedom, but they'll happily tell you how to live your life.

And finally, the "Nostalgic Naysayer" wistfully longs for the "good old days" when measles was just a rite of passage and seatbelts were for wimps. They'll talk your ear off about how everything natural is safe, blissfully ignoring that arsenic, uranium, and rattlesnake venom are also all-natural and decidedly not safe.

Together, they form a symphony of silliness, an ensemble of error. Their followers hang on to every tweet, share, and post, as if they're nuggets of wisdom rather than fool's gold. These charismatic characters don't just stretch the truth; they put it through a taffy puller, offering a distorted reality that's as dangerous as it is sticky.

Their methods are a blend of fear-mongering, nostalgia, and pseudoscience, all wrapped up in a glossy package of social media savvy. They've got the art of going viral down to a science - a perverse irony, given their disdain for actual science.

But fear not, for every charlatan there's a chorus of real experts, tirelessly debunking and demystifying. The key to not getting swept away in the current of craziness is to keep your wits about you, your sources checked, and your patience plentiful. After all, in the grand theatre of vaccine misinformation, the best defence is a good sense of humour and an even better BS detector.

Combating Misinformation Without Losing Your Marbles

Alright, my fellow truth-warriors, strap on your helmets and sharpen your wits - it's time to delve into the delicate art of debating with the anti-vax legion without going absolutely bonkers.

First off, remember the golden rule: Don't play chess with pigeons. They'll just knock over the pieces, crap on the board, and strut around like they won it all. So, when you're wading into the murky waters of misinformation, keep your expectations as low as a limbo stick at a contortionist convention.

Next, arm yourself with facts, but don't be surprised if they're about as welcome as a fart in a spacesuit. You'll present peer-reviewed studies, and they'll counter with a meme that looks like it was created by a toddler on a sugar rush. It's like bringing a gun to a pillow fight - the tools of engagement are just not the same.

Now, if you do decide to engage, here's a handy-dandy strategy: The Socratic Smackdown. Instead of telling them they're wrong, ask questions. "Interesting point, Karen, but can you explain how essential oils trump decades of medical research?"

Watch them twist faster than a balloon animal at a kid's party.

Should you find yourself getting sucked into a vortex of absurdity, channel your inner Zen master. Take deep breaths. Remember, you can lead a horse to water, but you can't make it think. Some folks would rather drink the Kool-Aid than the clear, scientific H2O you're offering.

And for the love of sanity, pick your battles like you pick your nose - privately and with intention. Not every comment section is your personal Colosseum. Sometimes, the thumbs-down is mightier than the sword.

As you navigate these choppy conversations, wear your sarcasm shield, and wield your wit sword, but keep your humour holster strapped tight. A well-timed joke can disarm better than a debate bomb. It's about opening minds, not winning points. You're not trying to beat them in an argument; you're trying to win them over to reality's side.

Finally, end on a note of hope. Remember, for every die-hard denier, there's a silent observer taking it all in, and your reasoned, albeit snarky, responses might just be the nudge they need. Humour is a powerful ally; it can cut tension, illuminate truths, and make allies out of adversaries.

So, go forth and combat the nonsense with a smile on your face and a chuckle in your throat. After all, laughter is the best medicine - well, after vaccines, of course.

The Last Laugh In The Face Of Lunacy

And there we have it, a twisted tour through the funhouse mirrors of vaccine misinformation where the reflections of truth are as warped as a Salvador Dali clock. We've seen it all, from cowpox craziness to 5G paranoia, and have come out the other side with our brains battered but unbowed.

Let's recap the carnival of confusion with the eyes of a sceptic and the heart of a satirist. We began with the historical hodgepodge of fears, where vaccines were as misunderstood as a goth at a beach party. Then we waded through the digital swamp of misinformation, where facts are as elusive as a unicorn at a horse race. And who could forget the rogues' gallery of snake oil salesmen, peddling their wares with the charm of a reality TV villain?

We've learned that arguing with the anti-vax crowd can be like mud-wrestling with a pig; you both get dirty, but the pig likes it. Still, we soldier on, armed with the shield of sarcasm and the sword of snark, because, at the end of the day, this isn't just about scoring points in the comments section - it's about safeguarding the health of our species.

So let us rally, my fellow sentinels of science, with our banners of reason billowing proudly in the winds of wisdom. Let's march to the beat of evidence, not to the rhythm of retweets (or reposts, or whatever the hell Space Karen will decide to call them next). We stand on the shoulders of giants, from Pasteur to Salk, who handed us a world where smallpox is a history lesson, not a death sentence, and polio is a name, not a nightmare.

As we sign off, let's not forget that this isn't just a debate over data; it's a fight for our future. For every eye roll and facepalm, remember that the stakes are as high as they come. It's about life and limb, about the world we leave for the kiddos who are still figuring out that spaghetti doesn't really grow on trees.

Keep laughing, keep educating, and for science's sake, keep vaccinating. Because when the book of history slams shut on this chapter, let's make sure it tells the story of how reason and resilience won the day, with a little help from our friend, humour.

And remember, when the going gets weird, the weird turn pro. Stay pro, my friends

MICHAEL GOVE'S GRAND JETE: A SATIRICAL DANCE THROUGH TWO DECADES OF POLITICS

Strutting and Fretting Upon the Stage: The Highs and Lows of Gove's Political Choreography Unveiled

Dearest Mr Gove, I trust this post finds you well and in fine dancing form? I'm sure you're a busy man, and we have much to get through, so I'm going to avoid pussyfooting around and jump right in, shall I?

For nearly two decades now you've been tap-dancing on the tightrope of public opinion and politics with the finesse of a hippo in ballet shoes, so I feel it's time for a candid, no-bullshit review of your "illustrious" career, peppered with the kind of swearing that you've so richly earned and written in the language of one of your favourite hobbies:

Dancing like no one's watching (except we have been, and oh boy...)

Powdered Feet And Pivots Of Pretence

Let's start with a pirouette to a particularly piquant part of your political pas de deux: the Cocaine Tango. This delightful little number is where you, our virtuoso of virtue, stumbled into a waltz of hypocrisy that would make a saint swear.

Remember when you admitted to snorting cocaine in your younger days? Oh, the irony was as thick as a London fog. Here was a man, a bastion of conservatism, who penned screeds against drug use, only to be revealed as a past participant in the very vices he derided. It was like finding out the school principal was secretly the lead singer in a punk band.

This revelation was not just a tiny misstep; it was a full-blown faceplant onto the dance floor of duplicity. Your past drug use, juxtaposed with your staunch anti-drug rhetoric, was as jarring as a ballet dancer in a mosh pit. The public watched, jaws agape, as you cha-cha-cha'd around your previous statements with all the grace of a three-legged giraffe.

However, his wasn't just a toe-tapping tangle with your past; it was a full-blown boogie of bullshit. You, the man who would impose stringent rules on others, had a closet bursting with skeletons doing the conga.

And the grand finale of this dance? Your bid for the Tory leadership amidst this cocaine caper. As your past pirouetted into the public eye, you attempted to foxtrot over it with a confidence that was as misplaced as a fish on a bicycle. The result? Your leadership dreams evaporated faster than a line of coke on a hot dashboard.

Educational Jigs And Policy Jives

Now, let's boogie back to your time as the ringmaster of the Education circus, shall we? Oh, what a show it was! You, prancing around like a headless chicken in a barnyard, laying down reform after reform with the finesse of a chainsaw carving a turkey.

Your tenure as Education Secretary was less about nurturing the future of the nation and more about swinging a wrecking ball through the corridors of learning. You approached the delicate ecosystem of education like a toddler with a hammer – everything looked like a damned nail.

Remember the curriculum overhaul? You swirled through it like a tornado, tossing aside American classics in favour of a more “British” syllabus. Because God forbid our youth read about different cultures and perspectives or something that isn’t positively dripping in Union Jacks. Next, you'll be saying Shakespeare is too foreign because he uses too many big words.

Then there was your tango with teacher pensions and pay. You twirled into that dance with all the grace of a three-legged gazelle, slashing here, cutting there, leaving a trail of disgruntled educators in your wake - something we are still paying the price for. The strikes? A standing ovation from the teachers for your performance in making their lives harder than a granite sandwich.

And let’s not forget your quickstep with school inspections. Under your regime, Ofsted morphed into the Spanish Inquisition of the academic world. Surprise inspections? A brilliant idea! Nothing quite like a bit of panic and stress to keep the educators on their toes, eh?

Your time at the helm of education was akin to watching a one-man band fall down a flight of stairs - noisy, chaotic, and frankly, painful to witness. You turned our schools into a battleground where the casualties were common sense and the wellbeing of teachers and students alike.

In the end, you exited stage left with the education sector looking like a scene from a disaster movie - bedraggled, bewildered, and wondering what the actual fuck just happened.

Bravo, Mr. Gove, bravo. You managed to dance your way through the education sector leaving a legacy of controversy and consternation, one that we still feel to this day. Quite the performance, indeed.

Justice's Faltering Foxtrot

This chapter of your political ballet was like watching a penguin try to tap dance - awkward, uncoordinated, and frankly, just a little bit sad.

As Lord Chancellor and Justice Secretary, you sashayed into the legal realm with all the expertise of a chimpanzee conducting an orchestra. Your approach to legal aid reform was like trying to play Beethoven with a banjo - painfully out of tune and utterly misguided.

Remember your grand plans to cut legal aid? You pranced into that arena like a matador, but instead of a bull, you were facing the British justice system. Your cuts were as well-received as whoopee cushion in the Queen's throne room, leaving lawyers and defendants utterly bemused. Access to justice? More like access to the whims of a man who thought justice was a game of Monopoly.

Then there was your jive with prison reforms. Oh, what a sight! You twirled around, making grandiose statements about transforming prisons, but in reality, it was more akin to rearranging deck chairs on the Titanic. The overcrowding, the violence - under your watch, prisons turned into gladiator arenas, and you, sir, were fiddling while Rome burned.

Your tenure as Lord Chancellor was like watching someone do the moonwalk on a tightrope - misguided, precarious, and bound to end in a spectacle. The legal profession looked on in horror as you tap-danced over the very principles of justice and fairness.

And who can forget your infamous ban on books for prisoners? That move was about as popular as a mosquito in a nudist colony. Restricting access to books - because nothing says rehabilitation like depriving people of education and escape.

In the end, your time as Lord Chancellor was an interpretive dance of confusion and controversy. You left the stage with the legal system more tangled than a set of Christmas lights, and with your credibility as mangled as a twist in a B-grade plot.

Eurosceptic Shuffle And Westminster Waltz

Oh, Mr Gove, where do we even begin? (As a note,

please do brace yourself, because this bit is going to be lengthy as there is much fuck aboutery afoot!)

Let's not be coy about your role in the sad, sordid, sorry saga, a dance as calamitous as it was cunning. Remember when you claimed the UK held all the cards post-Brexit? That was like betting your house on a three-legged horse in the Grand National. The reality? More like holding a hand of jokers while playing chess.

The aftermath of your Brexit ballet is a spectacle of loss and disillusionment. Trade? It's dropped like a lead balloon at a helium party, thanks to those pesky trade barriers you glossed over. The UK's economic hardship, already a sore point, has been amplified by your grand Brexit plan, leaving industries and individuals alike grappling with the fallout. It's like you set the house on fire and then tried to sell us water at a premium.

And let's talk about the environmental protections you promised would remain intact. Those promises evaporated faster than a puddle in the Sahara. We're now watching environmental standards get shredded faster than a confidential document in a politician's office. It's like promising to protect a rainforest, then handing out chainsaws at the entrance.

Losing access to the Erasmus programme? That's a cultural and educational self-sabotage of epic proportions. It's as if you took the concept of "broadening horizons" and gave it a lobotomy.

The opportunities for growth, connection, and learning, once readily available, are now as distant as a mirage in your Brexit desert.

Your Brexit dance was more than a political misstep; it was a frenzied fuck up of a foxtrot into uncertainty. The UK, once a vital part of a powerful European bloc, now finds itself an awkward, solitary figure on the global stage, all thanks to your choreography. It's like promising a luxury cruise and delivering a dinghy with a hole in it.

In your Brexit tango, you promised the stars and delivered a black hole. The UK, grappling with the consequences of your pied piper routine, is left wondering louder every day if the tune was worth the dance. As for holding all the cards? The only thing you've held is a mirror to the consequences of political hubris.

Eco-Two-Step And Policy Pirouettes

Now, Let's shimmy over to the murky waters of your stint as the Environment Secretary, shall we? It was like watching a fox being put in charge of a hen house's environmental policy. Under your watch, pledges for green policy seemed to bloom like spring flowers, only to wither under the scorching sun of actual implementation.

You spoke of "Green Brexit" with the enthusiasm of a preacher in a revival tent, promising environmental utopia. Yet, what did we see? Environmental policies left flapping in the wind like an abandoned kite. There were promises of sustainable fishing that somehow managed to smell fishier than the catch of the day. And let's not forget the air quality strategy - or should I say, the lack thereof? It seemed to vanish like clean air in a smog cloud.

It's as if your approach to environmental protection was akin to a child in a sweet shop - lots of excitement, but very little thought for the aftermath. The legacy you've left in environmental policy is a patchwork quilt of unfulfilled promises and policies as robust as a chocolate fireguard.

And through it all, there you were, Mr. Gove, a chameleon in a suit, blending into the background whenever accountability came knocking. Your environmental dance was less a waltz and more a stumble in the dark, leaving those who truly care about our planet's future to pick up the pieces.

In the grand ballet of your political career, your turn as Environment Secretary was perhaps one of the most bewildering performances. Full of sound and fury, signifying, well... not very much in the end. A performance that promised so much yet delivered so little, like a firework that fizzles out before the grand finale.

Bricklaying Beats And Developmental Disasters

Now, let's hustle over to your foray into the Housing and Communities portfolio, shall we? Here you were, like a crane swinging through a conservatory, promising to rebuild the housing landscape. But what did we get? More bluster than bricks, more rhetoric than roofs.

Remember your grand plans for social housing reform? It was like promising a housing revolution and delivering a stack of Monopoly houses - colourful, sure, but utterly useless in reality. Your commitment to building affordable homes for the masses rang hollow, echoing like a promise shouted into an empty construction site.

And then there's your handling of the cladding crisis post-Grenfell. You vowed to make buildings safe, to protect lives. Yet, for many, the reality has been an agonising waltz of uncertainty and fear. Your assurances were as flimsy as the unsafe cladding they were meant to replace – a dance of delay and deflection.

Under your watch, the housing sector has been a jigsaw with missing pieces - a picture of broken promises and half-completed plans. You promised a symphony of construction and delivered a cacophony of confusion. It's as though you were trying to build a castle on quicksand, each policy sinking before it could take hold.

And who could forget your theatrical display over housing standards? It was like watching someone trying to juggle flaming torches, only to end up singeing their own eyebrows. The standards you espoused often seemed more aligned with the interests of property developers than the people in desperate need of homes.

In the housing arena, your performance was less a masterful ballet and more a clumsy tap dance around the issues. Residents and communities were left waiting in the wings, their hopes for affordable, safe homes dimmed by the spotlight of your political aspirations.

So, there you have it, Mr. Gove. In the grand theatre of your political career, your time in housing and communities was yet another act where the script promised much, but the delivery stumbled, leaving the audience - the British public - waiting for a finale that never came.

Linguistic Twists And Dialectical Disasters

Now, to move onto something with just a slight bit more levity before I have a coronary at all the cock ups that I've had to remind myself of... Accents. Oh, Mr Gove, the accents! When it comes to imitating dialects, you've got all the subtlety and nuance of a foghorn at a chess tournament. Your attempts at accents are like a cat walking on a piano - sure, it makes noise, but it's hardly music to anyone's ears.

Remember your infamous venture into the

Scottish accent? It was like listening to a mangled mash-up of Groundskeeper Willie and a malfunctioning bagpipe. Not only was it as painful as stepping on Lego with bare feet, but it also had all the authenticity of a three-pound note. Watching you butcher the Scottish brogue was like witnessing a linguistic car crash in slow motion - you just couldn't look away, no matter how much you wanted to (and oh, how we all desperately wanted to!).

And who could forget your equally tragic stab at a rap? That moment when you decided to channel your inner Eminem and gave us a rendition that was more Vanilla Ice on a bad day. It was the auditory equivalent of dad-dancing at a wedding - awkward, embarrassing, and leaving everyone watching just a little bit mortified.

But let's not stop there. Your attempt at an American accent was another gem in your crown of vocal disasters. It was as convincing as a toupee in a hurricane, and about as comfortable as a porcupine in a balloon factory. Your twang was so off the mark, it left actual Americans wondering if they'd somehow forgotten how their own accent sounded.

Curtain Call For A Political Pantomime

As we reach the finale of this scathing serenade to your political ballet, let's be honest. Your career has been a kaleidoscope of blunders, a cavalcade of missteps choreographed to the tune of opportunism, hypocrisy and self-preservation.

From your cocaine waltz and educational tango to your Brexit breakdance and environmental two-step, each act has been a testament to your remarkable ability to dance around issues with the grace of a drunken elephant. You've played the part of the jester in the court of politics, capering about with a mischievous glee that's as infuriating as it is astonishing.

But here's the rub: while your political dance has been entertaining in its absurdity, the consequences of your actions have been anything but amusing. Each pirouette and plié has left its mark, not just on the marble floors of Westminster, but on the very fabric of our society. Your follies in education, Brexit, housing, and the environment have been more than mere political footnotes; they've been full-blown chapters in the book of governmental cock-ups and they have left us with broken services and a legacy of utter decline.

In a way, Mr. Gove, you're like a Shakespearean character brought to life, a tragicomic figure who bumbles and stumbles through the corridors of power, leaving chaos in your wake. But unlike a character in a play, your actions have real-world impacts, affecting millions who look to their leaders for guidance, not gaffes.

As I pen this missive, I can't help but wonder: what's next in the Michael Gove show? What new dance will you conjure up in your ceaseless, desperate quest for political relevance? Whatever it may be, one thing's for certain - it'll be a performance worth watching, if only for the sheer spectacle of it all.

But let's not kid ourselves. The laughter and eye-rolls you elicit are tinged with a sense of foreboding, a recognition that behind the farce lies a deeper malaise in our political system - one where ambition often trumps integrity, and the dance of power takes precedence over the needs of the people.

So, Mr. Gove, as you take your bow, know this: the audience may be applauding, but it's not necessarily in admiration. It's a clap of exasperation, a slow, deliberate applause for a politician who's become the embodiment of political theatre – captivating, yes, but ultimately, a performance that leaves us yearning for something more, something better.

DEFENDING OUR RIGHTS: THE BATTLE AGAINST ABANDONING THE ECHR

Understanding the European Convention on Human Rights, Its Impact on UK Law, and the Dire Consequences of Rejecting It

Gather around, you lovely lot, because today we're diving headfirst into a legal maelstrom that's got the political pundits in a tizzy and the right-wing Tories frothing at the mouth like rabid dogs. We're talking about the European Convention on Human Rights (ECHR) – a document that's about as thrilling as watching paint dry, but with the power to keep the government's grubby hands off our basic freedoms.

Now, before you tune out, thinking this is just another snooze-fest about legal jargon, let me tell you, this issue is as crucial as it gets. The ECHR isn't just some paper tiger. It's the big guns of human rights in Europe, and it's got a direct line to how we live our lives here in the UK. It's the referee in the boxing ring of politics, making sure the government doesn't land below-the-belt punches on us, the public.

But here's the kicker: the right flank of our Tory Party, led by none other than our Prime Miniature, Rishi Sunak, is itching to give this referee the boot. Why? Because apparently, the ECHR is the bane of their existence, the kryptonite to their Superman, hindering their noble quest to "stop the boats." It's like they believe waving goodbye to the ECHR will magically solve immigration issues. I mean, come on! That's like trying to fix a leaky tap by blowing up the whole bloody building.

So, let's strap in and dissect this beast. We're going to unravel what the ECHR actually is (spoiler: it's more than just legalese), how it's stitched into the fabric of our law like a patch on a well-worn pair of jeans, and what the implications could be if we decide to give it the old heave-ho. Spoiler alert: it's a grim picture, like a Picasso painting during his blue period – depressing as hell.

Stay tuned, because we're about to embark on a journey through the twisted labyrinth of legalities and political posturing. And I promise, by the end of this, you'll be more clued up about your rights than those Tory toffs are about the price of a pint of milk.

The Echr Unpacked: More Than Just Legal Jargon

So, what in the name of all that is holy is the ECHR? Let's strip away the legalese and get down to the nitty-gritty. Picture this: It's the late 1940s, Europe's still reeling from the horrors of World War II, and there's a collective realisation that "Hey, maybe we should make sure this sort of clusterfuck doesn't happen again." Enter the ECHR, birthed in 1950 as Europe's promise to itself to uphold basic human decency.

The ECHR isn't some lofty philosophical manifesto. It's a legally binding treaty that lays down the law on human rights. We're talking about the heavy hitters here - the right to life, freedom from being tortured, freedom of expression, and the right to a fair trial. It's the Avengers of human rights, assembled to fight the tyranny of governments going rogue on their people.

But here's where it gets interesting for us Brits. The ECHR isn't some foreign imposition; it's a set of standards the UK had a hand in creating. Yup, you heard that right. Winston Churchill, that bulldog of Britishness, a man that can leave Boris Johnson speechless, was a cheerleader for this thing. So, when I hear Tories moaning about European overreach, I can't help but chuckle, shake my head and kick a wall. Jesus, lads and lasses, we practically wrote the bloody playbook!

The ECHR also established the European Court of Human Rights in Strasbourg - not exactly a holiday destination, but crucial, nonetheless. This court is like the headmaster's office for countries playing truant on human rights. If you think the government's trampling over your rights, this is where you can take your grievances. And yes, Brits have done this, about 563 times up to 2021 - and won 327 times where it appears that our government was in fact playing fuckabouts with our rights (with at least one issue of fuckery found)! It's our "get out of jail free" card when the government tries to lock us up in the proverbial Monopoly hotel of injustice.

Now, the Tories' beef with the ECHR seems to revolve around immigration, specifically their inability to deport people as freely as they'd like on planes to Rwanda. They're making it out like the ECHR is the big bad wolf huffing and puffing at our sovereign borders. But let's be clear: this isn't about border control. It's about our rights, the rights the ECHR protects. Without it, we're just one step away from a government that can do whatever the hell it likes, and are you really sure you want to give Jonathan Gullis unlimited power over anything more complex than discarded crisp packet?

In the next section, we'll delve into how the ECHR is woven into the very fabric of UK law, and why ripping it out is akin to pulling the thread that unravels the whole sweater. Stay tuned, it's about to get even more interesting.

The Echr And Uk Law: A Tangled Web Of Rights And Regulations

Now, let's get into the meat of it – how the ECHR is stitched into the very fabric of UK law. This isn't just a case of international law playing nice with domestic rules. Oh no, it's far more entwined than that. It's like ivy clinging to a tree – you can't remove it without a hell of a lot of effort and probably damaging the tree in the process.

In 1998, the UK passed the Human Rights Act, which essentially brought the ECHR into British law. It's like we copied and pasted the ECHR directly into our legal system. This means that the principles of the ECHR aren't just nice ideas from across the Channel; they're part and parcel of our laws here. The Act requires all public bodies in the UK - yes, including the government - to treat people according to the rights laid out in the ECHR.

Now, why is this important? Because it means that you, me, and the bloke down the pub have a recourse if we feel our rights have been trampled on. Before the Human Rights Act, if you wanted to challenge a rights violation, you'd have to trot off to Strasbourg with your little pack of files in tow. Now, you can bring that fight right to the UK courts. It's like having a guard dog in your own backyard instead of relying on a distant relative's hound to protect you.

But here's where the Tories come in with their scissors, ready to snip away. Their gripe is that the ECHR limits their ability to make laws as they please, especially around hot-button issues like immigration. It's like they're annoyed that they can't play god without someone calling them out. They argue that leaving the ECHR would give us back control over our laws. But what they're conveniently forgetting (or more likely ignoring) is that those laws include our fundamental rights and freedoms.

If the UK ditches the ECHR, it's not just about losing a set of legal guidelines. It's about losing a safety net that protects us from our government going full-tilt authoritarian. Without the ECHR, there's less to stop them from passing laws that could infringe on our freedom of speech, privacy, or even our right to protest. It's like taking off the stabilisers and hoping the government doesn't veer us straight into oncoming traffic (let's keep in mind the 49 days of Truss madness, shall we?).

The Nitty-Gritty: Rights Afforded By The Echr

Okay, so, let's roll up our sleeves and delve into the juicy bits - the actual rights the ECHR bestows upon us. These aren't just abstract concepts; they're the bedrock of a society that doesn't treat its citizens like disposable napkins. So, what does this mighty document protect?

Let's break it down:

1. **Right to Life (Article 2)**: This one's a no-brainer. The ECHR says, "Hey, you can't just go around snuffing out lives." It's the ultimate "don't kill people" rule, but with legal teeth. It also obligates governments to investigate suspicious deaths and deaths in custody - a crucial check on state power.
2. **Prohibition of Torture (Article 3)**: This isn't just about forbidding medieval-style torture chambers. It covers any inhuman or degrading treatment. Think about it - it's 2023, not the Dark Ages. You'd think we wouldn't need to spell this out, but here we are.
3. **Right to Liberty and Security (Article 5)**: This means you can't be thrown in the clink without a good reason. It's the right not to be arbitrarily detained, ensuring that if you're arrested, there's a legitimate, legal reason for it - not just because

someone in power doesn't like your face.

4. **Right to a Fair Trial (Article 6)**: Ever heard the phrase "innocent until proven guilty"? That's this right in a nutshell. It's about having a fair, public hearing, by an independent and impartial tribunal. No kangaroo courts or trials by media here (despite what Jacob Rees-Mogg would like you to believe).

5. **Right to Respect for Private and Family Life (Article 8)**: This one says your private and family life is, well, private. It's a guard against Big Brother-style surveillance and ensures the sanctity of your home and correspondence. In today's digital age, this right is more important than ever.

6. **Freedom of Thought, Conscience, and Religion (Article 9)**: Basically, you're free to believe whatever you want, whether it's in a flying spaghetti monster or nothing at all. And you can practice your religion or belief - within reason, of course.

7. **Freedom of Expression (Article 10)**: This is a biggie - the right to say what you think, without the government slapping a gag order on you. It's not just about protecting your right to rant on Twitter; it's about safeguarding the press, protestors, and even artists.

8. **Freedom of Assembly and Association (Article 11)**: Want to protest? Form a union? Join a chess club? This right protects all that. It's about being able to come together with others

and collectively express, promote, pursue, and defend common interests, and it's one I'm sure our current government is truly chomping at the bit to get rid of if we look at the events of this past weekend during Armistice Day.

9. **Prohibition of Discrimination (Article 14)**: This one ties the whole thing together. It says you can't be denied any of the above rights based on sex, race, colour, language, religion, political opinion, or any other similar criteria. It's the "play fair" rule of human rights.

These rights are the toolkit for preventing a government from going full dystopian on us. They're not just nice-to-haves; they're must-haves. Ditching the ECHR means these rights would no longer be directly enforceable in UK courts. It's like unpinning the safety net while walking a tightrope - sure, you might not fall, but do you really want to take that chance?

Now, next up, we'll take a grim walk through the hypothetical wasteland of a UK without the ECHR. Spoiler alert: it's less "Sunlit Uplands" and more "Town at the End of Democracy Lane".

A Grim Look At The Uk Without The Echr

Now, let's paint a picture of a not-so-rosy future where the UK decides to wave goodbye to the ECHR. It's like envisioning a party after the keg's run dry – bleak, disappointing, and with a bunch of people wondering why they're still there. Without the ECHR, we're looking at a landscape where the government can redraw the map of our rights with fewer checks and balances.

First off, let's talk about the right to privacy. Say ta-ta to safeguards against unwarranted surveillance. Without the ECHR, the government could snoop through your emails, listen in on your phone calls, or track your movements with fewer legal hurdles. It's a step towards a surveillance state where Big Brother isn't just watching you; he's breathing down your neck.

Freedom of expression? That would take a hit too. Without the ECHR, laws limiting what you can say, write, or even post online could be enacted with less resistance. It's like walking on a tightrope over a pit of censorship - one false step, and you're in the soup. This isn't just about protecting your right to rant about the government; it's about safeguarding our democracy's very lifeblood.

And what about those due process rights? Without the ECHR, the fairness of trials and the treatment of detainees could be compromised. We could see an erosion of the "innocent until proven guilty" principle, leading us down a slippery slope towards miscarriages of justice.

Now, don't even get me started on discrimination. Without the ECHR's prohibition on discrimination, laws and policies could become more biased, whether it's based on race, gender, religion, or sexual orientation. It's like stepping back in time to when inequality was the norm, not the exception.

Let's not forget the impact on those most vulnerable. Without the ECHR, policies regarding asylum seekers, refugees, and immigrants could become harsher, less humane. It's a path leading away from compassion and understanding, towards a colder, more callous society (and I will remind you, we've just had a Home Secretary gleefully try to ban tents for the homeless - imagine how much Cruella could get away with if she's truly let loose).

In short, ditching the ECHR isn't just about changing a few laws here and there; it's about fundamentally altering the landscape of our rights and freedoms. It's about moving from a society that respects and protects individual liberties, to one where those liberties are increasingly conditional, contingent on the whims of those in power.

So, as we listen to the Tories banging the drum to leave the ECHR, remember what's at stake. It's not just about sovereignty or border control; it's about the kind of country we want to live in. Do we want a UK that upholds the principles of justice, fairness, and equality? Or one where those principles are discarded like yesterday's newspaper? The choice might soon be in our hands, and it's one we'll have to live with for generations to come.

The Call To Action - Protecting Our Rights

So here we are, standing at the crossroads (again), facing a future that could very well be stripped of the safeguards afforded by the ECHR. But let's not descend into despair just yet. Instead, let's talk about what we can do, how we can stand up and fight for the rights that define us, and our society.

Firstly, it's about getting clued up. Knowledge is power, my friends. The more we understand about what the ECHR does for us, the better equipped we are to defend it. It's like going into battle; you wouldn't march into the fray without knowing what you're fighting for, would you? Spread the word, shout it from the rooftops, and make sure everyone knows what's at stake.

Next, it's time to make our voices heard. Write to your MP, light up their inboxes, flood their desks with letters demanding they protect our rights. Remember, these MPs work for us, not the other way around. It's high time they're reminded of that. We need to turn up at town hall meetings, join protests, and participate in demonstrations. It's about showing strength in numbers, a united front that says, "We will not stand for this."

And don't forget the power of the ballot box.

Voting isn't just a right; it's a weapon in our arsenal for change. We need to support and vote for candidates who pledge to uphold and protect our human rights. It's time to be strategic about our votes, to see them as chess moves in the bigger game of safeguarding our freedoms.

Moreover, we need to support human rights organizations. These groups are on the front lines, battling it out in courts, holding governments to account, and they need all the support they can get. Whether it's through donations, volunteering, or simply amplifying their message, every little bit helps.

Finally, let's talk about solidarity. This isn't just a fight for lawyers and politicians; it's a fight for all of us. Every one of us, regardless of our backgrounds, professions, or beliefs, has a stake in this. We need to stand together, unified in our commitment to a society that respects and protects the rights of all its members.

The road ahead may be fraught with challenges, but remember – history is full of moments when the will of the people has triumphed over the machinations of the few. This is our moment, our fight. So, let's gear up, stand tall, and fight to ensure that our rights, enshrined in the ECHR, remain intact. Because if we don't, who will?

In the end, it's about the kind of legacy we want to leave behind. A legacy of complacency and loss? Or one of resistance and victory in the face of adversity? The choice is ours, and it's one we need to make now, before it's too late.

UNRAVELLING THE ECHR SPAGHETTI: A NO-BULL GUIDE TO THE RIGHTS RODEO

From Sovereignty Shenanigans to Economic Tall Tales - Slicing Through the Hot Air Balloon of ECHR Myths

Ladies, Gents, and everyone who can spot a political circus from a mile away, in our previous chapter, we discussed the ECHR and why it's a rather important club to be a part of. Today I'm going to continue this little tour of the

ECHR, but this time focusing on some of the things we're hearing about the European Court of Human Rights that, to be perfectly frank, belong straight in the bin (you can choose whichever of your seven bins you would like to put it into).

So, our beloved Tory government took a proper nosedive in the Supreme Court over their "send 'em to Rwanda" game plan. No surprises there, right? But what did surprise me (or maybe not) was the knee-jerk chorus screaming to ditch the European Convention on Human Rights (ECHR) faster than a rat deserting a sinking ship.

Now, before we all jump on the "dump the ECHR" bandwagon, let's take a breath and do a bit of myth-busting. Seems like there's a load of codswallop floating around about what the ECHR is and isn't, and it's about time we sifted through this muck.

Get ready for a rollercoaster ride through the land of misinformation, where we'll tackle the top arguments for giving the ECHR the boot. Expect some colourful metaphors, a smidge of coarse language (because why the hell not?), and a good dollop of cold, hard facts.

Strap in, folks. It's going to be a bumpy ride.

Control Freaks Anonymous: Debunking The Sovereignty Sob Story

Alright, let's wade into the murky waters of

the first argument: that leaving the ECHR will somehow magically restore the UK's sovereignty, like pulling a rabbit out of a hat. Proponents of this view are hollering that we need to yank back control of our laws and borders from the clutches of the ECHR. Sounds dramatic, doesn't it?

Here's the snag, though: The ECHR isn't some villainous overlord dictating our laws. It's more like a friendly neighbourhood watch, ensuring we don't trample over basic human rights while we go about our business. The ECHR complements our legal system, reinforcing values that, surprise, surprise, were partly drafted by British legal beagles. So, this isn’t about stealing back control; it’s about living up to standards we helped set.

Those banging the drum of sovereignty seem to forget that the ECHR has been part of our landscape since the 50s. It's been the backbone of some landmark rulings, like upholding LGBTQ + rights and safeguarding privacy. Tossing it aside isn't just a slap in the face to these achievements; it's like trying to unscramble an egg – messy and frankly, impossible.

Think about it: The ECHR’s influence is woven into our legal tapestry. Yanking it out isn't going to give us more control; it'll leave a gaping hole in our human rights protections. It's akin to chopping off your nose to spite your face, then realizing you’ve got nowhere to put your glasses.

So, when they say it's about sovereignty, it's really

about opting out of a system that holds us to a higher standard. And let's be honest, in the current political climate, we need all the help we can get to maintain some semblance of decency and accountability.

Next up, we'll dive into the murky claim that the ECHR is a playground for criminals and lawbreakers. Spoiler alert: it's as shaky as a three-legged table at a tap-dancing contest.

Cry Wolf: The "Echr As A Criminal's Paradise" Bullshittery

Time to slice through Argument Number Two like a hot knife through butter: the notion that the ECHR is nothing but a fancy playground for criminals and ne'er-do-wells. The cry is that these rascals are using the ECHR to play the system like a fiddle, twisting human rights to dodge justice.

Hold your horses, though. This argument is about as stable as a three legged antelope on a hot tin roof. Sure, there might be a few crafty characters who try to game the system - every garden's got a few weeds, after all. But to paint the entire ECHR as a loophole for crooks is like saying the Internet is only good for cat videos and conspiracy theories (tempting, but not true).

Most people protected by the ECHR are regular Joes, Janes, Johns and Rubys – folks like you and me, just trying to ensure they're not getting the short end of the stick. It's about safeguarding the little guy from being steamrolled by Big Brother, not giving a get-out-of-jail-free card to villains.

Ditching the ECHR based on this argument is akin to throwing the baby out with the bathwater, then chucking the tub, the soap, and the rubber duck for good measure. It's an overreaction that risks undermining the rights of millions to catch a handful of baddies.

Let's face it: the problem isn't the ECHR itself, but how it's sometimes manipulated. We need a scalpel, not a sledgehammer, to refine and address these issues. Blaming the ECHR for every legal loophole is like blaming your hammer for hitting your thumb - it's not the tool's fault if it's misused.

Next, we'll tackle the thorny issue of immigration and borders – another favourite punching bag for the ECHR critics. Get ready for a reality check that's as welcome as a fart in a spacesuit.

Borderline Nonsense: The Echr Immigration Bogeyman

Next up we dive into Argument Three: the ECHR is the big bad wolf at the door of our immigration and border control. The pitch is that this pesky human rights guardian is the reason we can't have nice things, like iron-clad borders and an immigration system as watertight as a duck's arse.

Here's the rub: portraying the ECHR as the villain

in our immigration saga is about as accurate as a drunk darts player. Yes, immigration is a complex beast, and no one's saying it's as simple as a fairy tale. But the idea that the ECHR is stopping us from managing our borders is like blaming your diet failures on the existence of chocolate – convenient, but a bit of a stretch.

The ECHR doesn't tie our hands behind our backs; it ensures we don't go full medieval on people seeking refuge. It's about balancing control with compassion, something that seems to be in short supply lately. Scrapping the ECHR won't magically fix our immigration issues. It's not a silver bullet; it's more like shooting ourselves in the foot.

Human rights aren't the enemy of effective border control. We can have strong borders and still treat people with dignity – the two aren't mutually exclusive. Suggesting we dump the ECHR to strengthen our borders is like saying we should get rid of traffic laws to reduce congestion. Sure, you might get to work faster, but you're likely to cause a ten-car pileup on the way.

Next up, we'll untangle the often-misunderstood relationship between the ECHR and the EU. Spoiler: they're about as related as I am to royalty (and no, I'm not the long-lost prince of anywhere).

Eu-Phobia: The Great Echr-Eu Mix-Up

Now, let's clear up Argument Four, a tangled web of

confusion: the ECHR is an EU overlord, and post-Brexit, we should cut it loose like a bad Tinder date. This one's a doozy, folks, and it's about as grounded in reality as a unicorn at a tea party.

Here's the deal: the ECHR is not, I repeat, not an EU institution. This is a mix-up on par with confusing Star Wars with Star Trek - it's bound to get you some eye-rolls. The ECHR is the brainchild of the Council of Europe, which, fun fact, includes countries like Russia and Turkey, who are definitely not doing the EU tango.

Equating Brexit with ditching the ECHR is like saying you need to stop eating baguettes because you quit French class. They're not even in the same cookbook. The ECHR was around before our tiff with the EU and operates independently of it. Ditching it post-Brexit isn't a power move; it's a facepalm moment of epic proportions.

The ECHR underpins our human rights legislation. It's the bedrock of fairness and decency in our legal system. Throwing it away just because we've left the EU is like throwing out your TV because you don't like the news - it's a knee-jerk reaction that solves precisely nothing.

As A Side Note, Do We Really Trust The Tories With Our Human Rights? Really?

Ah, you say, but the government says that we will

write *our very own* laws to protect our human rights, and they will be as British as a pork pie and a lager on a hot summer's day.

But, before we get carried away, let's ponder a rather prickly question: Do we really trust the Tories, the architects of austerity, Thatcherism, COVID calamities, and anti-protest movements, to pen a new Human Rights Act that genuinely protects us? It's like asking a fox to design the henhouse security system.

Think about it. This is the same party that brought us the Poll Tax, the bedroom tax, and a slew of policies that, let's be honest, weren't exactly oozing with compassion. Their track record in protecting the vulnerable and upholding individual liberties is about as reliable as wax fire door.

The COVID-19 response? A cocktail of blunders and U-turns. And let's not forget the policing bill, which seems less about keeping the peace and more about muzzling dissent. If history teaches us anything, it's that this lot and human rights are as compatible as oil and water.

Rewriting the Human Rights Act is no small feat. It requires a delicate balance, a deep understanding of the law, and above all, a commitment to fairness and justice. Based on past performances, trusting this government to handle such a task is like trusting a sack of angry vipers to babysit a clutch of rabbits - the outcome is likely to be a mess.

So, before we cheer on the prospect of a brand-new Human Rights Act penned by the current government, let's take a hard look at their report card. It's speckled with enough red marks to make even the most optimistic among us pause and consider: Is this really the crew we want steering our rights ship?

Cutting Through The Echr Fog Of War

So, there we have it, a myth-busting journey through the thicket of arguments for ditching the ECHR. It's been a wild ride, akin to navigating a hedge maze blindfolded.

Let's be blunt - the push to leave the ECHR feels less about genuine concern for British sovereignty, security, or prosperity, and more like a political sideshow, a distraction with a dash of fear-mongering. It's like using a firework display to cover up a fender bender.

The ECHR is not the bogeyman some make it out to be. It's not about losing control, being soft on crime, hindering immigration policies, being shackled to the EU, or economic doom and gloom. It's about standing by the principles that define us – fairness, decency, and a commitment to upholding basic human rights.

Ditching the ECHR would be a step backward, a leap into a future where rights are a gamble, not a guarantee. It's time we saw through the smoke and mirrors, the political spin, and recognized the ECHR for what it truly is – a cornerstone of our modern, democratic society.

In the end, it's not just about laws and treaties; it's about the kind of country we want to be. Do we choose fear, isolation, and regression, or do we stand for dignity, fairness, and progress? I know where I stand, and I hope you do too.

Stay sharp, stay informed, and let's keep fighting the good fight.

WELCOME BACK, LORD CAMERON: AN UNLIKELY ENCORE IN FOREIGN AFFAIRS

From Brexit to Greensill, an Ode to the Baron of Chipping Norton's Storied Return to the Political Limelight

Dearest Lord Cameron, Baron of Chipping Norton, (Well, that is an unpleasant mouthful!) Welcome to the carnival, Lord David Cameron, or should I say, Foreign

Secretary – a title as surprising as finding a teetotaller at Oktoberfest. Your appointment by our diminutive Prime Miniature, Rishi Sunak, reeks of desperation, akin to scraping not just the bottom, but the underside of the barrel. And truly, the irony is utterly delicious! The man who set our international relations ablaze with the Brexit bonfire is now in charge of dousing the flames. It's like handing a pyromaniac a fire extinguisher and hoping for the best. One can't help but chuckle at the thought of you, the architect of one of the most divisive and shambolic episodes in British political history, now steering the ship of diplomacy. This, Lord Cameron, is either a stroke of twisted genius or a farce so grand it deserves its own West End run.

Austerity: When Tightening Belts Choked Society

Before we delve into the labyrinth of your latest appointment, Lord Cameron, let's rewind to the hallmark of your premiership: austerity. Austerity - that grand experiment where the nation was the lab rat, and the poorest bore the brunt of the scalpel. This was no mere tightening of belts but a full-fledged gutting of social services, the echoes of which still reverberate in the hollowed-out communities across our isles.

Under your watch, austerity was painted as an

unavoidable sacrifice, a necessary evil to balance the books. But let's call a spade a spade, shall we? It was an ideological choice, one that preyed on the vulnerable while the upper crust remained comfortably cushioned, the impact of which veered wide of the people you surround yourself with. The cuts to public services were not just numbers on a spreadsheet; they were lifelines snatched away from those clinging to the edges of society.

The impact? Where to begin, Lord Cameron. The NHS, that jewel in our crown, was left gasping for air. Social care was slashed, leaving the elderly, and disabled in a lurch. Education, housing, and local government services faced the guillotine, and the welfare system was gutted like a fish. The result was a society more divided, with the chasm between the haves and the have-nots yawning wider than ever.

And let's not forget, this was not just an economic policy; it was a social one. The narrative of "strivers vs. skivers" vilified the poor, painting them as lazy freeloaders, conveniently ignoring the systemic barriers that keep them shackled. The rise in food banks, child poverty, and homelessness - these are your legacy, the indelible marks of a policy that took from the many to spare the few.

We are left in a country in which 3.8 million people are living in destitution - a word that leaves me cold.

Now, as you step into the role of Foreign Secretary, one must wonder: will the echoes of austerity follow you? Will the same principles that dictated domestic policy now shape our international relations? An utterly chilling thought indeed.

This message on austerity, Lord Cameron, is a reminder of the path you've trodden, a path littered with the casualties of your policies. It's a legacy that, much like your return to the political stage, many of us are struggling to reconcile with.

Brexit - The Gift That Keeps On Giving

Now, on to Brexit, the pièce de résistance of your legacy, Lord Cameron. It was like watching someone light a match to see if the gas tank was full - and, oh boy, was it ever! The referendum, your "gift" to the nation, turned out to be the equivalent of gifting a grenade to a toddler. The sheer brilliance of it! Who needs stable governance when you can have chaos, confusion, and a dash of regret?

The irony is thicker than the English fog that now you, of all people, are tasked with navigating the intricacies of international diplomacy. The same man who thought it wise to gamble the country's future on a referendum, now in charge of mending the fences you joyfully smashed with a sledgehammer. It's like putting the fox that previously ravished the chickens in charge of the hen house, then wondering why all the birds are nervous and giving a sharp side eye.

Your Brexit brainchild has been like watching a car crash in slow motion - only the car is the UK, and the driver is a blindfolded aristocrat with an outdated map. And as the nation still reels from the impact, we find ourselves entrusting our global standing to the very architect of our isolation. It's akin to asking the iceberg to please kindly reassemble the Titanic.

Truly, your return to the political stage as Foreign Secretary under Prime Miniature Sunak is a testament to the enduring power of the old boys' network. It's not what you know, but who you know - and apparently, whom you've gone to school with. Bravo, Lord Cameron, for this masterful display of elite acrobatics.

Greensill Capital: A Masterclass In Post-Power Decorum

Post-premiership life! It's a time for memoirs, speaking engagements, and if you're feeling particularly adventurous, a bit of light lobbying. Enter Greensill Capital, the stage for your next act, Lord Cameron. Your involvement with Greensill was like watching an artful dodger at work, only the art was rather lost in translation. The seamless transition from leading a country to texting ministers for favours was... well, let's call it "unconventional".

Your escapades with Greensill Capital could be a masterclass in "What Not to Do After Downing Street". Your relentless lobbying efforts on behalf of Greensill, an endeavour that seemed more like a desperate attempt at a payday than any noble cause, were as subtle as a sledgehammer. The texts, the calls - it was like watching a lovesick (slightly horny, let's face it) teenager trying to get a date to whatever the Eton equivalent is of a school dance. Only in this case, the school dance was a billion-pound bailout, and the date was the British taxpayer.

Let's not forget the fallout. The investigation that followed was akin to opening Pandora's box, only instead of evils, it was filled with cringe-worthy text messages and questionable judgement calls. Your actions turned the spotlight on the very fabric of Westminster's corridors of power, revealing a tapestry woven with threads of cronyism and backdoor deals.

In a way, Lord Cameron, you've become the poster child for the very "elite" you once commanded, a shining example of the revolving door between politics and business. It's a stark reminder that power, like fine wine, can intoxicate, and sometimes, leave a bitter aftertaste.

Lord Cameron's Return: A Foreign

Concept In Diplomacy

And now, the big reveal your grand re-entry into the political circus, Lord Cameron, as Foreign Secretary. The irony is so thick you could cut it with a knife. The man who lit the fuse of Brexit, now in charge of mending fences and playing nice with the neighbours. It's like asking a bull to repair the china shop it just utterly demolished.

One might think this is a well-crafted joke, a satirical piece perhaps, but no, it's the reality we find ourselves in. The appointment reeks of the old boys' club mentality, where positions of power are less about capability and more about chumming it up at the club. It's like a game of musical chairs played by the elite, and you, Lord Cameron, have found your seat again, much to the bewildered amusement of us mere mortals.

Your tenure as PM was marked by a certain detachment from the common pulse, a trait one hopes has been tempered by time. But who are we kidding? This is politics, British style, where the unexpected becomes the norm, and the absurd, routine.

As you step into this role, one can only wonder what awaits. Will you be the statesman who mends bridges, or the architect of further chaos? Only time will tell. But rest assured, Lord Cameron, all eyes are on you, some in disbelief, others in bemusement, as you embark on this latest chapter of your illustrious career. Godspeed, and may the odds be ever in your favour (they usually are, aren't they?).

Curtain Call: An Encore Of Irony And Infamy

Well, Lord Cameron, as we wrap up this letter, let's not mince words. Your journey from PM to a controversial post-premiership life, and now to Foreign Secretary, reads like a script rejected for being too far-fetched. But here we are, watching this drama unfold in real-time.

Your legacy, thus far, has been a mixed bag of austerity, Brexit chaos, and Greensill scandal - not exactly the stuff of legend, unless we're talking about cautionary tales. And yet, in a turn of events that defies logic (but apparently not politics), you've been handed the reins of our international relations.

In your new role, you have a chance to rewrite some wrongs, to perhaps leave a mark that won't be remembered with a wince. But let's not hold our breaths. If history has taught us anything, it's that the leopard seldom changes its spots, especially when it's comfortably nestled in the upper echelons of power.

So, as you settle into your new office, perhaps ponder on this: power is a fleeting thing, but the legacy it leaves behind can last for eternity. Here's to hoping your second act in the political theatre is more statesman and less Greek tragedy. But who are we kidding? This is British politics. Tragedy and farce are never too far apart.

In sarcastic camaraderie and with a watchful eye, I bid you good luck, Lord Cameron.

You're going to need it.

SUNAK'S FIVE-FINGER DISCOUNT: PILFERING OUR FUTURE WITH EMPTY PROMISES

Unveiling the Hollow Echoes of Old Pledges and the Farce of New "Priorities" in Sunak's Political Playbook

Well, it’s that time again - another day, another set of priorities from our Prime Miniature, Rishi Sunak. It's like watching a child flick the light switch on and off, hoping to illuminate something new, but it's the same old room every time.

Here we are, staring down the barrel of his old and new five-point plans, a rollercoaster of underwhelming rehashes and wishful thinking masquerading as policy. It's a real smorgasbord of political déjà vu, with each “priority” paraded out like a tired show pony, prancing to the same old tune.

In the spirit of masochism, or maybe just sheer bloody-mindedness, I'm diving headfirst into this mire. We'll tear apart the old priorities, a mishmash of half-arsed attempts and blatant failures, and dissect the new ones, which, spoiler alert, are about as inspiring as a wet weekend in Wigan.

So, buckle up, folks. We're in for a bumpy ride through Sunak's Wonderland, where reality is optional, and hope is a currency as inflated as his ego. Let's see if we can find some semblance of sense in this circus of political spin. And who knows? Maybe we'll unearth a nugget of truth beneath all the bullshit.

Echo Chamber Of Ineptitude: Sunak's Broken Record Routine

Every night, it's the same bloody story. I jerk awake, drenched in a cold sweat, my mind racing with the relentless, maddening mantra of Sunak's priorities: "Halve inflation, grow the economy, reduce debt, cut waiting lists, stop the boats." It's like being haunted by a political poltergeist, an endless echo bouncing around my skull until reality mercifully seeps in, and I can only let out a defeated, exasperated groan.

This isn't governance; it's a goddamn Groundhog Day of political posturing. These priorities, repeated ad nauseam, have become the white noise of our current political discourse, a tiresome loop that's as uninspiring as it is infuriating. It's like Sunak's got a broken jukebox in his head, playing the same track over and over, expecting us to dance along like everything's hunky-dory. Well, we're not bloody dancing, Rishi.

The issue isn't the country; it's the bloke fumbling at the controls. Sunak's approach to policy is akin to a clueless gamer mashing buttons, hoping for a win. His strategy? Turn the country off and on again, and if that doesn't work, just repeat the same old tired lines. But here's the kicker - the problem is PICNIC. Problem In Chair, Not In

Computer. Our Prime Miniature seems oblivious to the fact that the country isn't a machine that can be rebooted with yet another new set of buzzwords.

What we're witnessing is a carousel of incompetence, spinning us round and round with these "priorities" while the real issues keep piling up, unaddressed and festering. It's high time someone told Sunak that this isn't a game, and his monotonous, recycled promises aren't going to cut it. We're sick of the repetition, the lack of originality, and, frankly, the audacity to think we wouldn't notice.

So, here's to dissecting this political pantomime, one overused, underwhelming priority at a time. Let's see what's behind the curtain of Sunak's grand illusion - if anything at all.

The Hall Of Shame: Dissecting Sunak's Fumbled Fiascos

Let's start with the old promises, shall we? The stale bread of Sunak's political feast.

1. **Halving Inflation:** Yes, inflation has halved, but let's not pop the champagne just yet. This was expected, a natural ebb and flow, not some financial wizardry by our Prime Miniature. And let's face it, this "achievement" came with a hefty price tag for Joe, Jane and Josiah

Public, thanks to rising interest rates. Essentially, the common folk have been left to foot the bill while Sunak takes a victory lap. Bravo!

2. **Growing The Economy:** Talk about a pie in the sky! The economy isn't expected to show any growth until 2025. Meanwhile, our fearless leader is probably still trying to find the "Economy Growth" button on his dashboard. Spoiler: *It doesn't exist.*
3. **Decrease Debt:** Now, this is a real knee-slapper. Under Sunak's watchful eye, debt has been anything but decreased. It's like watching a gambler in Vegas - the more they lose, the more they bet, hoping the next round will be their big win. Spoiler: *It won't be.*
4. **Cutting NHS Waiting Lists:** An absolute disaster. These waiting lists aren't just numbers; they're people – real people with real problems, languishing in a system that's been systematically gutted and neglected. Steve Barclay, while at the helm, treated this like a minor inconvenience rather than the crisis it is. Industrial action has been a massive driver in this issue - and the governments approach? Ostrich the fuck out of it and hope it goes away.
5. **Stop The Boats:** The one area where

there's been some movement, but not enough to warrant a pat on the back that Mr Long Socks Sunak so desperately wants. The boats are down, thanks largely to agreements with countries like Albania, but Sunak's fixation with the laughable Rwanda policy and the stagnant backlog of asylum applications reveal a level of incompetence that's almost impressive.

In summary, Sunak's old priorities are a smorgasbord of failed policies, half-measures, and missed opportunities. It's like watching a chef promise a gourmet meal and then serve up reheated leftovers. Uninspiring, unpalatable, and utterly disappointing.

Reheated Rubbish: Sunak's Latest Serving Of Half-Baked Hogwash

Now, onto the 'new' priorities. If you thought the old ones were a hodgepodge of wishful thinking, brace yourself for this round of Sunak's political bingo.

1. **Reducing Debt:** We're off to a stellar start, aren't we? Sunak's track record on debt reduction is about as impressive as a knitted condom. The debt situation under his watch is akin to trying to bail out a sinking ship with a teaspoon.

Ambitious, but ultimately futile.

2. **Cutting Tax:** Oh, the classic Tory carrot! But let's be real, cutting taxes for the sake of it, especially in areas like inheritance tax, is a slap in the face to the average Brit. People don't mind paying taxes, provided they see returns in public services. But where's the return when our public services are practically non-existent? Seriously, where the actual fuck has all our tax money gone?
3. **Securing Energy:** Broad and vague, like a magician's promise. Sunak's idea of securing energy involves new licences for oil and gas drilling, a plan with the foresight of a mole in broad daylight. Instead of investing in sustainable, green energy, we're digging deeper into fossil fuels. Talk about missing the mark by a country mile!
4. **Backing British Business:** A lovely sentiment if it didn't reek of cronyism. Backing business should mean all British businesses, not just those in the inner circle of the Tory club. It's time to support the underdogs, the local heroes, not just the big players who already have a seat at the table.
5. **World-Class Education:** A goal as lofty as it is hollow under the current

regime. Our schools are crumbling, both literally and metaphorically. World-class education in buildings that might as well have “Danger: Falling Debris” signs? That's not just ironic; it's tragic.

In essence, Sunak's new priorities feel like the old ones, just reheated and served with a side of empty promises. It's the same song, just a different verse. Our Prime Miniature seems to be playing a game of political Whack-A-Mole, swinging aimlessly, hoping to hit something substantial. But alas, it's all just a spectacle, a show of motion without progress, sound without fury, signifying nothing but the same old, tired political theatre.

In A Parallel Universe: Visions Of A Competent Government

In the land of political fantasies where Sunak’s priorities roam free, there exists a parallel universe where realistic and practical priorities could make a genuine difference. Let’s take a stroll through this alternate reality and envision what could be if our government focused on truly meaningful and achievable goals:

1. **Strengthening Public Services:** Instead of the perpetual austerity waltz, how about we actually invest in our public services? This means pumping funds into the NHS, education, and social

care. It's not rocket science; it's basic governance. People want to see their tax money working for them, not disappearing into the black hole of government inefficiency.

2. **Genuine Economic Growth Strategies:** Growth doesn't just sprout overnight like a mushroom after rain. It needs nurturing, careful planning, and investment in areas that will yield long-term benefits. This includes supporting small and medium-sized enterprises, incentivizing innovation, and investing in green technology to future-proof our economy.
3. **Comprehensive Mental Health Support:** With mental health crises skyrocketing, this should be front and centre of any government's agenda. We need accessible, well-funded mental health services, community support programs, and an end to the stigma surrounding mental health issues.
4. **Real Solutions to the Housing Crisis:** It's time to address the elephant in the room - the absurd housing market. This means building affordable housing, regulating the rental market, and ensuring that owning or renting a home isn't just a distant dream for the many.

5. **A Green and Sustainable Future:** Instead of empty rhetoric, let's see tangible action towards sustainability. This includes serious investment in renewable energy, green public transportation, and policies that encourage sustainable practices across all sectors.
6. **Fostering Social Equality:** Last but certainly not least, we need a government that actively works towards reducing inequality. This means addressing the gender pay gap, fighting racial discrimination, and ensuring that everyone, regardless of their background, has a fair shot at success.

In this realm of realism, priorities are more than just buzzwords; they're actionable plans with clear outcomes and benefits. They're about making a tangible difference in people's lives, not just scoring political points or creating soundbites for the evening news. If only our current leaders would take a page from this book, we might just see a Britain that works for everyone, not just the few at the top.

The Emperor Has No Clothes: Exposing Sunak's Naked Incompetence

So here we are, at the end of this whirlwind

tour of Sunak's bullshit bingo – his old and new "priorities". It's been a wild ride of empty promises and half-arsed attempts that would be laughable if it weren't so bloody tragic for the country.

The original set of priorities were about as effective as a rubber beak on a woodpecker. Halving inflation? A fluke more than a feat. Growing the economy? More like watching paint dry. Cutting NHS waiting lists? A fucking pipe dream. And don't get me started on the "stop the boats" mantra – it's like trying to plug a dam with a wad of chewing gum.

And now, the new priorities. What a load of recycled, regurgitated crap. Reducing debt? He's already ballsed that up. Cutting tax? Great, just what we need, more breaks for the rich. Securing energy? Sure, if you mean drilling us into oblivion. Backing British business? Yeah, as long as it's his mates'. World-class education? Tell that to the kids learning in crumbling schools.

What we need isn't another round of these piss-poor priorities. We need actual, meaningful action. It's high time for a government that doesn't just spout the same old tired lines but gets down to the nitty-gritty of what this country really needs.

In short, it's time for Sunak and his cronies to stop the endless cycle of bullshit and start doing something - anything - that actually makes a tangible difference. Enough of the rehearsed rhetoric. We're sick of it. It's time to roll up the sleeves and get to fucking work.

PRINCIPLES OR PRETENCE? DISSECTING THE NOLAN STANDARDS IN TODAY'S POLITICAL CIRCUS

A Deeper Look at the Gap Between High Ideals and Low Politics in the UK Government

Ah, the Nolan Principles - those seven holy commandments of public office that seem as elusive in today's political circus as a truthful statement in The Daily Mail. Dreamed up in the mid-90s, a time when political scandals were as rife as a bad rash, these principles were supposed to steer our dear politicians away from the cesspools of corruption and disgrace. But let's call a spade a spade, shall we? Lately, these principles seem more like a bloody joke than a guiding light.

From Home Secretaries criminalising kindness (because, God forbid, we show empathy to the homeless), to Prime Ministers pulling policies out of their arses faster than rabbits from a magician's hat, the current state of UK politics is a far cry from what ol' Lord Nolan had envisioned. And don't even get me started on the MPs who moonlight as TV stars on right-wing channels, wearing their bias like a badge of bloody honour.

In this piece, I'm going to take a no-bullshit look at these Nolan Principles, dissecting their history, importance, and just how spectacularly our current bunch of leaders are failing at them.

A Whirlwind Tour Through The Nolan

Principles' Not-So-Glorious Past

Let's time travel back to the mid-90s, shall we? The UK political scene was about as clean as a pub floor after a Friday night brawl. Scandals were blooming like mould in a damp flat, with MPs getting caught left, right, and centre for all sorts of shenanigans and fuckery. We're talking about accepting cash for questions and other cheeky misdeeds that would make even a seasoned con artist blush.

Enter stage left: Lord Nolan. He's tasked with cleaning up this mess, a Herculean task if there ever was one. In 1995, he chairs the Committee on Standards in Public Life and, et voila, out come the Seven Principles of Public Life. These were supposed to be the Holy Grail of ethical conduct for public officials - a simple guide to not being a complete disgrace while in office.

The Nolan Principles, in a nutshell, are a set of behavioural commandments: Selflessness (think Robin Hood, not King John), Integrity (keeping it clean, no backhanders), Objectivity (facts over favourites), Accountability (own your decisions, even the crap ones), Openness (transparency is key, secrets are a no-go), Honesty (tell the truth, even when it stings), and Leadership (be the role model, not the cautionary tale).

These guidelines were meant to usher in an era of squeaky-clean governance. But, as history shows, they've often been regarded with the same seriousness as a “please do not walk on the grass” sign at a rock festival.

Why The Nolan Principles Matter More Than Ever

Alright, let’s talk turkey about why these Nolan Principles are not just some fancy words to be framed and hung in a dusty corridor of Westminster. They are the moral compass for our public life. Without them, we’re just a ship in a storm without a rudder, and right now, that storm's looking like a bloody hurricane.

First off, **“Selflessness”** isn't about throwing a few quid at charity and calling it a day. It's about making decisions that benefit the public, not your wallet or your mate's holiday home in the Bahamas. It's about putting the country's needs before your own, something that seems to have been forgotten in the corridors of power.

Then we've got **“Integrity”**, a word that seems to be as rare in politics as a unicorn in Trafalgar Square. It’s about not being swayed by the shiny baubles of power and money. Can we honestly say our current leaders are passing this test with flying colours? I wouldn’t bet my last pint on it.

“Objectivity“ is next in line, and it's about making decisions based on facts, not favours or who you went to Eton with. Decisions should be made for the good of all, not just the few with the right connections.

"Accountability" – oh, this is a good one. Leaders should be able to stand up and say, "Yes, I did that, and here's why..." Not scurry away like roaches when the lights come on. Our government leaders seem to have developed an allergy to this principle.

"Openness" isn't just about not telling porkies; it's about being transparent. That means not just revealing what you want when it's convenient. It means letting the public see the workings behind decisions, warts and all.

"Honesty" – now, there's a principle that's been taking a beating. It's simple: tell the truth. Don't dress up failures as successes or pretend like bad decisions were actually 4D chess moves.

Lastly, **"Leadership"**. This is about setting an example. It's about walking the walk, not just talking the talk. It's about showing respect, even to those who disagree with you, not mocking them on social media like a bloody playground bully.

In an ideal world, our leaders would embody these principles like superheroes wear capes. But in reality, we're seeing more villains than heroes. The importance of these principles? It's about trust, respect, and having a government that we can believe in, not one that treats these values like a joke.

In the current climate, where trust in our government is about as low as it can get, these principles aren't just important; they're essential.

They're the difference between a democracy that works for everyone and a playground for the privileged few. Without them, we're just spectators at a very bad pantomime, and let me tell you, it's not a fun show.

A Parade Of Principle-Breaking: Real-Life Examples From Our Current Government

Now, let's march into the hall of shame where the breaking of the Nolan Principles is almost an art form. We're looking at you, current Tory government. Here's a rogue's gallery of examples that make you wonder if they've ever even heard of these principles:

- **Suella Braverman's Homeless Tent Fiasco**: Our Home Secretary, who thought criminalising tents for the homeless and fining charities was a stroke of genius. **Selflessness**? More like heartlessness.
- **Rishi Sunak's Make-Believe Policies**: Then we have our Prime Minister, conjuring policies out of thin air to backpedal on Net Zero Targets. I guess **"Honesty"** and **"Openness"** were out to lunch that day.
- **Therese Coffey's Hush-Hush on Benefits**

Impact: The Secretary of State for Work and Pensions playing hide-and-seek with reports on benefit changes. Spoiler alert: **"Accountability"** and **"Openness"** are not playing.

- **The GB News and Talk TV Saga**: A cluster of MPs moonlighting on right-wing TV shows, bagging extra cash. Do **"Integrity"** and **"Objectivity"** ring any bell, folks?
- **Rishi Sunak's Russian Family Ties**: While Russia faces sanctions, our PM's family business ties raise more than a few eyebrows. **"Integrity"**, are you still with us?
- **Brendan Clarke-Smith's Social Media Antics**: An MP mocking a woman with mental health issues on social media. **"Leadership"** and **"Respect"** just left the chat.

These are just the tip of the iceberg. It's like they've taken the Nolan Principles, used them as a dartboard, and are having a laugh at our expense. The scary part? This isn't a complete list - it's only a snapshot of how far off course we've veered. Going through all the issues we see on a daily basis would be enough material for me to write a book about!

It boils down to the fact that these principles aren't just guidelines; they're the foundation of trust in our government. And right now, that foundation looks as solid as a sandcastle at high tide.

Conclusion

As we draw the curtains on this sardonic little theatre of the absurd, let’s reflect on the Nolan Principles and our current government's performance. It's been a bit of a rough ride through a landscape where principles often seem more like suggestions than rules.

The Nolan Principles, conceived as a moral compass for public office, have turned into a sort of mythical creature in the current political climate - often talked about but seldom seen. Selflessness, integrity, objectivity, accountability, openness, honesty, and leadership - these words should define the heart and soul of public service. Instead, they've become distant echoes in the halls of power, drowned out by the cacophony of self-interest and political manoeuvring.

The dissonance between these ideals and the reality is more than just disappointing; it's a bloody farce. It's like watching a pantomime where the actors have forgotten their lines, except it’s not funny because the consequences are real and often devastating.

What's needed isn't just a return to these principles; it's a total reboot of the system that allows such flagrant deviations. It's about time we held our leaders to the standards they pledged to uphold. We need leaders who don't just pay lip service to these principles but embody them, leaders who understand that public service is a privilege, not a platform for personal gain.

In the end, the Nolan Principles should be more than words on a page; they should be the very foundation of our democracy. Until we see that level of commitment, we'll keep sharpening our pens, ready to call out the bullshit wherever we see it. Because let's face it, at the rate we're going, there's going to be plenty more to write about.

WELCOME TO THE UK: WHERE MIGRANTS PAY A FORTUNE TO KEEP US AFLOAT AND POLITICIANS PAY LIP SERVICE

Exploring the untold story of migrant contributions and debunking political myths – it's time to set the record straight on immigration in the UK.

Well, blow me down with a feather! Suella Braverman, our recently departed Home Secretary, has been at it again with a tweet that's as subtle as a sledgehammer in her usual style of rhetoric. She's rattling the cages about immigration, claiming the UK's packed in an extra million folks in two years – that's a whole bloody Birmingham, she says! The panic buttons are being hammered: housing, the NHS, schools, wages, and - God forbid - community cohesion are all apparently going to hell in a handbasket. Her solution? Clamp down on the influx with good old Brexit's toolbox. We're talking caps on net migration, jacking up salary thresholds, and slamming the door on dependents.

But here's the rub: how much of this is just political theatrics, and how much is grounded in the cold, hard facts? In this piece, we're going to sift through the bull and get down to brass tacks. We'll dive headfirst into the latest migration stats, particularly that juicy "Long-term international migration, provisional year ending June 2023" report. Expect a no-holds-barred look at the supposed strain on our systems, the real kick in the teeth that Braverman's policies could be, and the financial muscle that migrants actually flex in this little island's economy.

So, buckle up, it's going to be a bumpy ride through the reality of immigration in the UK. We'll cut through the crap and lay it all out – because when it comes to making policies that affect real lives, the last thing we need is to be led up the garden path by scaremongering and half-truths.

The Misleading Nature Of "Pressure On Systems"

Let's talk rather directly about this "pressure on systems" malarkey. Braverman's been banging the drum, claiming our green and pleasant land is about to buckle under the weight of newcomers. Housing, healthcare, schools – you name it, it's apparently on the brink of collapse. But hold your horses; is it really a case of too many cooks spoiling the broth, or is there more to the story?

First off, let's get one thing straight: a fair chunk of these so-called "pressure-inducing" migrants are actually the ones keeping the show on the road. Take the NHS, for example. If we threw out every Jenny Foreigner in the scrubs and lab coats, we'd be up the creek without a paddle. These folks aren't just filling in the gaps; they're vital cogs in the machine. And it's not just healthcare. Industries across the board are propped up by migrant talent - from engineering whizz-kids to the wizards of the IT world.

Now, about housing. Sure, more people means more demand for roofs over heads. But let's not pretend like the housing crisis is a new tune. It's an old record that's been playing long before the "great migrant influx" of Braverman's nightmares. It's more a case of dilly-dallying in policy, investment and utter failure by the Tory Government than a migrant-made melodrama.

And as for schools and wages - come on, let's cut the theatrics. Migrant workers contribute to the economy, paying taxes that fund these very institutions. They're not the bogeyman here; they're part of the backbone that keeps the UK standing.

In a nutshell, it's a bit rich to paint migrants as the villains of the piece, especially when they're more like the unsung heroes. It's about time we flipped the script and gave credit where it's bloody well due.

The Humanitarian And Practical Consequences Of Limiting Dependents

Now, let's wade into the murky waters of Braverman's brainwave to limit dependents on all visas. Sounds like a plan hatched on the back of a fag packet, doesn't it? It's not just tight-fisted; it's bloody cruel. Imagine telling Mr. Pereira, our brainy engineer from my tweet this morning, "Sure, come fix our bridges, but leave your family behind." That's not just harsh; it's heartless.

Let's talk about the humanitarian angle first. Families are not optional accessories; they're the whole bloody kit and caboodle. Splitting them up for the sake of some hard-line immigration stance is about as compassionate as a brick. It wreaks havoc on mental health, not just for the folks coming over, but for the families left in limbo. It's not rocket science to see that happy, settled workers are better for everyone - they're more productive, more engaged, and let's face it, less likely to up sticks if they've got their loved ones with them.

Then there's the practical side of this bonkers idea. We're already scraping the barrel to find skilled workers in key sectors. Now add the "no family allowed" rule and see how many takers you get. It's like trying to sell a car with no seats and wondering why there are no buyers.

Limiting dependents might sound like a nifty solution in the fantasy world where every migrant is a single, footloose individual. But back here on planet Earth, it's a policy that could backfire spectacularly. It's not just about numbers on a spreadsheet; it's about real people making tough decisions about their lives. And let's not forget, today's dependent child could be tomorrow's top surgeon, tech guru, or, dare I say, a politician with a bit more sense.

In short, this isn't just a bad idea; it's a recipe for

disaster – socially, economically, and morally. It's high time we looked at immigration as more than just a numbers game.

Economic Contributions Of Migrants: More Than Meets The Eye

Let's set the record straight about the economic side of things. It's time to put to bed the tired old trope that migrants are a drain on the system. Spoiler alert: they're not; in fact, they're often the ones keeping the British economy afloat.

This does not even touch on the absolutely exhorbitant costs of immigration and visas itself. Below, we'll discuss just how much it costs to get here, and believe me, it paints a stark picture of the financial odyssey these folks embark on. We're talking about shelling out a small fortune - north of £44,000! That's for visas, health surcharges, English tests, and a cornucopia of other expenses. This isn't chump change; it's a significant economic injection into our system. Every visa application, every health surcharge, every English test fee - that's all revenue. It's money that's buoying up the very services that are purportedly under strain from immigration.

And it doesn't stop at entry fees. Once here, migrants are paying taxes, propping up the economy, and often working jobs that are crying out for hands. From lifesavers in hospitals to the wizards behind the tech revolution, they're in the trenches, contributing their skills and paying their dues. They're not just participants in our economy; they're pillars of it.

But wait, there's more. Many of these hardworking souls aren't even eligible for benefits or social housing. They're here, contributing to the pot, but not taking a slice of the pie. That's the opposite of a burden; that's a boon. Every pound they earn and spend is a pound circulating in our economy, fuelling everything from local businesses to national infrastructure.

So, when you hear some politico or second rate journalist (Ms Pearson, ahem) spouting off about migrants draining resources, remember the facts. These aren't freeloaders; they're financially contributing members of society. They're not here for a free ride; they're paying their way - and then some. Without their contributions, we'd be in a tighter spot than a hedgehog in a balloon factory.

In essence, it's high time we started looking at immigration through a lens that sees the full spectrum of economic impact - the investments, the contributions, and the indispensable role migrants play in keeping the UK's economic engine running.

The Sneaky Salary Threshold Shuffle And Its Implications

Now, here comes the disgusting bit. I agree with Suella on something, which is enough to make me gag, but let me clarify before I must run to the loo to go empty my stomach and let's pull back the curtain on Braverman's clever little gambit: hiking up the salary threshold for immigration to £45k, while conveniently excluding health and social care workers.

Increasing the salary threshold isn't a daft idea. In fact, I'm on board with it, to an extent (gag). Why? Because it forces companies to put their money where their mouth is. If they're desperate for that top-notch talent from overseas, they better be ready to cough up the dough. And here's the kicker: it's not just the migrant workers who'd benefit from this. Oh no, it would set a precedent that could see our own British workforce enjoying a well-deserved pay bump. Everyone loves a raise, right?

But here's where the plot thickens: health and social care get a free pass from this salary surge. Now, why is that, I wonder? It's as clear as a bell on a sunny day - these sectors are notoriously underpaid. By carving them out of the salary hike, Braverman's inadvertently shining a spotlight on a grubby little secret: our health and social care workers are getting a raw deal.

This exclusion is where my hackles go up. It's an admission, plain as day, that these vital sectors are scraping the bottom of the pay barrel. It's a slap in the face to the hardworking folks in scrubs and care uniforms. This isn't just about immigration; it's about how we value those who look after our health and well-being. If we're saying £45k is a fair benchmark for skilled migrants, then by Jennifer, it should be a fair shake for the people keeping our hospitals and care homes running!

In essence, Braverman's sneaky salary shift is a double-edged sword. On one hand, it's a chance to push for better wages across the board. On the other, it's a glaring red flag that health and social care is undervalued and underpaid. It's about time we took a long, hard look at how we compensate the very people who patch us up and look after our elders.

So, while I grudgingly tip my hat to the idea of upping the salary ante, I can't help but scowl at the health and social care exemption. It's a sly move that speaks volumes about where our priorities lie - and where they desperately need to change.

Where To From Here?

So, what have we learned from diving headfirst into this immigration saga? Well, it's clear as day that the narrative being peddled by the likes of Braverman isn't just oversimplified; it's damn near misleading. Painting migrants as the bogeyman causing all our woes is not just lazy; it's dangerously inaccurate.

We've seen how the "pressure on systems" spiel is a bit of a red herring. Migrants aren't clogging up the works; they're often the grease keeping the gears turning. From the NHS to schools and beyond, they're essential, not extraneous. And let's not forget the financial side of things - these folks are paying through the nose just to get a foot in the door, and then they keep on contributing.

As for the proposed measures to restrict immigration, especially the heartless idea of limiting dependents - it's not just a bad move; it's a potentially disastrous one. It overlooks the basic humanity of keeping families together and ignores the practicalities of attracting skilled labour to our shores.

And finally, the economic argument. Migrants aren't draining our coffers; they're lining them. From the hefty fees they pay to enter and stay in the country to the taxes they contribute and the vital roles they fill in our workforce, their economic impact is overwhelmingly positive.

In a nutshell, it's high time we busted the myths and fear-mongering around immigration. The real picture is much more complex and, frankly, a lot more positive than certain politicians would have you believe. So, the next time someone starts banging the "immigration is bad" drum, remember the Pereiras of the world and the real story behind the headlines.

As for me, I'm off to enjoy a well-deserved

cuppa, and maybe, just maybe, a little less doom and gloom about our migrant pals. Here's to seeing things as they really are – complicated, challenging, but also chock-full of potential.

Cheers, and remember – keep your wits sharp and your heart open.

LEE ANDERSON: THE UNRULY MP IN THE SPOTLIGHT OF SCORN

A no-holds-barred dissection of one politician's journey through bullying, hypocrisy, and political farce.

Mr. Anderson, well, fuck me sideways, here we are, writing to you, Lee "30p" Anderson - the MP whose antics make a circus look like a bloody Quaker meeting. This isn't just any letter; consider it a love letter to your political "brilliance", penned out of sheer, unadulterated bewilderment at your capacity to embody the unholy trinity of bullying, duplicity, and hypocrisy.

I'm not here to mince words or blow smoke up your arse. No, we're diving headfirst into the cesspit of your political shenanigans. It's like peeling an onion of bullshit – each layer more pungent than the last, and by God, it brings tears to the eyes. And not the good kind, mind you. The kind that makes you question how the hell we ended up here, with you as a parliamentary representative.

Your unique brand of politics? It's like watching a car crash in slow motion – you know you shouldn't gawk, but bloody hell, it's hard to look away. You, Mr. Anderson, have turned the House of Commons into your personal playground of preposterousness, and frankly, it's as entertaining as it is horrifying.

So, let's not beat around the bush. I'll be calling out your antics with the candour of a northern grandmother who's just seen her grandkid drop a clanger at Sunday tea. We're going high-octane with our language here – no pedestrian 'darns' and 'hecks'. This is the big leagues of swearing, because, let's face it, your political track record deserves nothing less.

Buckle up, Mr. Anderson. We're about to embark on a journey through your political 'achievements', and I use that term as loosely as the morals in a brothel. It's time to hold up a mirror to your antics

– and don't worry, I'll make sure it's one of those funhouse mirrors, so you get the full, distorted effect of your actions.

Bullying 101 With Professor Anderson

On to the sordid saga of bullying, a subject in which you, sir, exhibit the finesse of a sledgehammer doing lacework. You treat tenants with the tenderness of a butcher at a vegan potluck. Your suggestion that "nuisance tenants" should be corralled into tents to pick spuds wasn't just a slap in the face; it was a full-on Glasgow kiss to the concept of compassion. If there was a line, you didn't just cross it – you took a piss on it while whistling "Rule Britannia".

Your social media escapades? It's like you're lobbing grenades in a playground and calling it banter. You prance around the Twittersphere swinging your insults like a drunken Morris dancer with a vendetta. It's like you've got a PhD in antagonism from the University of Arseholery, and you're here to give us your thesis.

And when it comes to migrants, your remarks are about as warm and welcoming as a fart in a lift. Telling desperate souls to "fuck off back to France" with the subtlety of a chainsaw carving a turkey - it's not just bullying, mate, it's broadcasting your narrow-mindedness in high-definition for the world to see. It's as if you're competing in the

Olympics of Offence, aiming for gold by punching down.

Let's face it, your idea of political discourse is as refined as a chimps' tea party. You've turned the act of bullying into performance art, where every parliamentary sitting seems to be your personal West End debut. The tragedy? The audience is forced to endure the show, with their taxes funding the production.

Your brand of bullying isn't just a series of gaffes; it's a relentless campaign that stomps on the downtrodden with the glee of a child in a muddy puddle, splashing filth without care. It's a shameless parade of your ego, where every strut seems designed to trample dignity underfoot.

So, we trudge through the quagmire of your political "contributions" - and make no mistake, it's a slog through a sewer channel of your own making. It's a grim tour, where each of your statements serves as a fetid landmark, a testament to your commitment to crassness and cruelty.

In Another Galaxy: Lee Anderson's Guide To The Common People

Out of touch? Mr. Anderson, you're so far removed from the pulse of the people, you might as well be broadcasting from the moon - and even then, I reckon the lunar rocks would offer a warmer reception. Your declarations of understanding the common struggle are about as convincing as a cardboard cut-out in a hurricane – they simply don't stand up.

Let's start with the infamous 30p meal fiasco, shall we? Your suggestion that meals could be whipped up for mere pennies wasn't just insulting – it was a slap in the face with a wet kipper to anyone who's had to count their coins just to make ends meet. It's the culinary equivalent of saying "let them eat cake", only you're serving up gruel and calling it gourmet.

And then we have your comments about nurses – hardworking individuals who've propped up this nation on their backs – using food banks. You claim it's a financial management issue. Really, Mr. Anderson? That's like saying the Titanic sank because it didn't steer clear of the ice – a masterpiece of missing the bloody point. Nurses shouldn't need food banks on a salary that should comfortably see them through.

Oh, and let's not forget your barometer of economic success: the bustling pubs. To hear you tell it, as long as the beer's flowing, the country's coffers must be overflowing. This pub logic of yours is a pint of nonsense. It's like measuring the health of the ocean by the number of fish in a single net. You're gauging the nation's wellbeing on the foot traffic in a chain tavern, ignoring the sobering reality outside those stained-glass windows.

Mr. Anderson, you're not just out of touch - you're out of your depth, spouting solutions as effective as a lacework condom. The people you claim to defend are wading through treacle thanks to policies you prop up and the actions of the government which you serve, and all you can offer is a pat on the back and a lecture on thriftiness? It's the kind of condescension one might expect from an aristocrat in a Dickens novel, not a 21st-century MP from Ashfield.

Your connection to the everyday Joe is as flimsy as the promises in a politician's manifesto - especially your own manifesto which is now beyond threadbare. Every time you open your gob to share these pearls of penny-pinching wisdom, you're not enlightening - you're enraging, fanning the flames of frustration in a public tired of being told to tighten belts by those who wouldn't know a budget if it bit them in the arse.

In the orchestra of out-of-touch elites, Mr. Anderson, you're the self-appointed conductor, leading a symphony of discord with every tone-deaf statement you trumpet. And trust me, the audience is not clamouring for an encore.

Hypocrisy Hoedown: Dancing With Double Standards

In the grand theatre of political farce, Mr. Anderson, your performance in the role of

Hypocrite-in-Chief is so stellar, it's a wonder you haven't been awarded a lifetime achievement award for services to duplicity. Your most breath-taking act? Leaping from Labour councillor to Tory MP with the grace of a cat burglar jumping ship as soon as the alarms blare. It's a wonder you didn't sprain an ankle with that deft display of opportunism, which would have been richly deserved, considering the load of self-interest you carted over with you.

Defection, Mr. Anderson, is a term too clinical for this switcheroo. Let's call it what it is - a Judas jig, a turncoat tango, a dance so self-serving it could make Narcissus himself blush. You've not just changed your coat; you've dyed it, flogged it, and paraded it around like a peacock at a bird show. And for what? A seat at the high table? A bit of silver to line those pockets? It's as if you spotted the winds of fortune changing and set your sails with all the subtlety of a brass band in a library.

Then there's the small matter of the £100k from your little GB News escapade, a tidy sum you pocket for spouting the very kind of codswallop you once criticised. After the Owen Patterson fiasco, you had the gall to point fingers at second incomes, only to be caught with your hand in the cookie jar. If hypocrisy were an Olympic sport, you'd be stood on the podium, gold medal hanging around your neck, the national anthem playing for your victory in vaulting values.

Calling a Parliamentary hearing into Boris Johnson's alleged misleading of parliament a "Kangaroo Court" was yet another stroke of your brush on the canvas of hypocrisy. You, the self-appointed arbiter of justice, dismissing the very processes you're meant to uphold. It's like a shark lecturing minnows on the virtues of vegetarianism, all while it's got a belly full of fish.

Your defection from Labour to Tory wasn't just a change of heart; it was a change of convenience, a switch flipped with the precision of a mercenary spotting a higher bidder. It wasn't for the people, it was for your own avarice and ambition, a power grab as transparent as a freshly cleaned window.

Your ability to flip-flop with such acrobatic agility is almost impressive. But let's call a spade a spade - it's not the flexibility of a gymnast we're seeing, it's the wriggling of a worm on a hook. Each twist and turn, a desperate squirm to inch closer to the apple of power, even if that apple is rotten to the core.

So, Mr. Anderson, take a bow. Your performance in the grand pantomime of hypocrisy has been one for the ages. But remember, the audience is wiser now, the applause you hear might just be the slow clap of realisation, as the penny drops, and the charade is laid bare for all to see.

The Art Of Political Illusion: Anderson's Masterpiece

Now, Mr. Anderson, let's talk about your little escapade in the theatre of the absurd, shall we? It's one thing to be a political chameleon, but another to be a bloody ventriloquist with your constituents. Remember the little caught on camera charade you put on? Getting a mate to play the part of a disillusioned Labour voter, all while you were mic'd up like a reality TV star hoping for a prime-time slot.

That wasn't just a fib, it was a full-on fucking pantomime with you as the lead in a one-man show titled "The Great Pretender". A bit of advice, free of charge: if you're going to play the puppet master, at least have the decency to not get caught with your hand up the puppet's arse on national telly.

You tried to sell us a dodgy second-hand car of a political stunt, hoping no one would notice it was missing a bloody engine. But oh, they noticed, because the bonnet was up, and all that was there was you, grinning like a cat that got the cream, except the cream was off, and the cat was out of the bag.

This wasn't just bending the truth; it was snapping it in half and setting it on fire. A campaign tactic as transparent as cling film, and about as sticky. It's stunts like this that give politics a bad name, making voters more jaded than a recycled beer bottle.

In short, it was a cock-up of colossal proportions,

a masterclass in how not to win hearts and minds, unless you're aiming to win them in the same way a car crash wins rubberneckers. It takes a special kind of brazen to pull a fast one under the spotlight, and you, Mr. Anderson, are nothing if not special.

Lee Anderson's Guide To Trashing Political Dialogue

In the grand cacophony of political discourse, Mr. Anderson, you've managed to hit a note so sour, it makes vinegar taste like sugar water. Your antics aren't just a blip on the radar; they're a bloody tornado, tearing through the already fragile landscape of public trust in politics.

You see, every time you open your gob to spout something that reeks of hypocrisy, or when you serve up a lie so bold it could have its own postcode, you chip away at the bedrock of our democracy. People aren't just rolling their eyes; they're questioning the integrity of the entire bloody system. And who can blame them? It's like watching a dog chase its tail - amusing for a split second, then just plain sad.

Your brand of politicking, if we can grace it with such a term, is the kind that turns debates into brawls and discussion into diatribes. It's the kind that wouldn't know subtlety if it came dressed as a neon sign. The impact? It's about as constructive as a wrecking ball in a crystal chandelier emporium, leaving us to sweep up the shards of what could have been productive conversation.

And let's not kid ourselves, these aren't mere ripples in a pond; this is a tsunami of bollocks that's flooding the airwaves, drowning out reason and common sense. It's a masterclass in how to make a shambles of discourse, a veritable "how-to" guide on turning the political arena into a circus, and not the kind with acrobats and fun clowns, but the kind where the lions have eaten the ringmaster.

In conclusion, the impact of your escapades is as beneficial to political discourse as a hole in a lifeboat. It's high time for a change in tune, lest the whole ship goes down with all hands-on deck, while you stand there holding the bloody drill.

Curtain Call: Bidding Adieu To The Absurdity

So, Mr. Anderson, as we pirouette to the conclusion of this less than poetic missive, it's clear you've turned parliamentary representation into a grim pantomime, where you're both the villain and the clown. Your antics, which smell fouler than a fishmonger's bin after a summer heatwave, leave a stench that not even the most fragrant of political Febreze can mask.

The sheer gall of your political tightrope act,

performed without a safety net of integrity or a semblance of shame, is enough to make a bishop kick in a stained-glass window. You've not just crossed the line; you've obliterated it with the force of a sledgehammer swinging down on the final nail in the coffin of decorum.

You parade about with the dignity of a rat in a top hat, spinning yarns that wouldn't hold up in a toddler's puppet show. It's a testament to the age-old adage that power can corrupt, but in your case, it's taken a detour through the circus and ended up in the sewer.

In a just world, you'd be held accountable at the stocks of public opinion, pelted not with rotten tomatoes, but with the decayed fruits of your own bitter harvest. But alas, we're left with the cacophony of your blunders ringing in our ears, a one-man band of bullshit playing to the tune of a populace that's bloody well tired of the noise.

So, here's a hearty "fuck you" with all the trimmings. May your political career be as short-lived as a mayfly with a death wish, and may the door hit you on the way and perhaps slam some sense and decorum into you. We're done with the farce, the charade, and the unadulterated codswallop that's become your trademark.

In the grand ledger of political legacies, your page will be a cautionary tale scrawled in crayon, a blaring warning siren for the next generation that this - this right here - is not how it's done. Not now, not ever.

And with that, we drop the mic on your pitiful performance. The curtain falls, the audience scatters, and the silence that follows is the most telling review of all.

WORDS AS WEAPONS: UNMASKING THE DANGEROUS RHETORIC IN THE COMMONS

Examining the Alarming Shift in Political Discourse - From "Disapply" to "Illegal Migrants", How Language Shapes Our Democracy

I have always held a deep reverence for the power of words. They are the tools of my trade (both this one and my day job), the weapons in my arsenal, and the keys to unlocking the hearts and minds of my readers. In the political arena, words are not just symbols of communication; they are instruments of influence, capable of shaping perceptions, moulding opinions, and swaying emotions. The potency of language in the hands of politicians can be a force for good, rallying communities towards unity and progress. However, it can also be a weapon of division, fear, and misinformation.

In recent times, we have witnessed a disturbing trend in the UK's political discourse. The language used in the House of Commons, particularly regarding sensitive issues like immigration and human rights, has taken a dangerous turn. Words are being twisted, manipulated, and weaponised, not to clarify or enlighten, but to obfuscate and mislead. This deliberate distortion of language is not just a threat to coherent debate; it's a direct assault on the very fabric of our democratic society.

In this piece, I'm going to dissect the recent comments of Mr. Jenrick and Mr. Clarke in the Commons. These statements, steeped in misleading terminology and dangerous rhetoric, are symptomatic of a broader issue – the reckless and irresponsible use of language by those in power. As we proceed, let's keep in mind the importance of precision and responsibility in our words, for they shape the world we live in and the future we are building.

Mr. Jenrick's Comments - A Dangerous Dance with Language

Mr. Jenrick's recent comments in the Commons are a masterclass in the misuse of language, a dangerous dance on the tightrope of political correctness that threatens to plunge us all into a pit of divisiveness and fear. Let's dissect his words, shall we?

Firstly, the term "illegal migrants" - bandied about with reckless abandon. It's crucial to understand that an "illegal migrant" is a person who enters a country without meeting legal requirements for residency or by overstaying a visa. Contrast this with refugees or asylum seekers, who flee their countries due to a well-founded fear of persecution and seek protection under international law. They're not breaking laws; they're exercising their rights under international conventions, to which the UK is a signatory. By labelling them as "illegal", Mr. Jenrick isn't just bending the truth; he's snapping it in half.

Now, I must of course mention his insistence

on Rwanda being the cornerstone of the government's migration policy. This is akin to placing a band-aid on a gunshot wound and calling it a cure. Declaring Rwanda a "safe country" unilaterally is not only ludicrous but also dangerously naive. It's an act of political sleight of hand, an attempt to distract from the failure to address the root causes of migration and refugee crises.

"...But the human tongue is a beast that few can master. It strains constantly to break out of its cage, and if it is not tamed, it will run wild and cause you grief." -Unknown

Mr. Jenrick's rhetoric is not merely misleading; it's inflammatory. By equating asylum seekers with criminals, he's not just playing fast and loose with language; he's igniting the flames of xenophobia and racism. It's a narrative that doesn't just border on fear-mongering; it dives headfirst into it. It's a toxic cocktail of misinformation and prejudice, served up in the guise of political posturing.

In summary, Mr. Jenrick's words are more than just irresponsible; they're a wilful distortion of reality, a deliberate attempt to recast refugees and asylum seekers in the role of villains. This isn't just about politics; it's about humanity. By twisting language to serve his agenda, Mr. Jenrick isn't just failing as a politician; he's failing as a human being.

Mr. Clarke's Comments - The Deceptive

Danger Of "Disapply"

When Mr. Clarke casually tosses around the word "disapply" in relation to the European Convention on Human Rights (ECHR) and refugee conventions, it might seem, at first glance, innocuously bureaucratic. Yet, this single term, seemingly benign, masks a seismic shift in policy - a shift that could easily rattle the very foundations of our democratic society.

The word "disapply" is a wolf in sheep's clothing. It sounds technical, almost mundane, but its implications are anything but. This is not about tweaking a minor policy detail; it's about sidestepping the fundamental rights that are the cornerstone of our legal system and our democratic values. By suggesting we can simply "disapply" parts of the ECHR, Mr. Clarke is advocating for a world where the protections we take for granted can be suspended at the government's whim. It's a world where the rule of law is not a steadfast principle but a malleable convenience.

Similarly, Suella Braverman's use of "notwithstanding" clauses in relation to the ECHR and the Human Rights Act (HRA) is equally troubling. This single word has the power to override key legal protections and bypass established legal norms. It's a legal bulldozer, capable of flattening the landscape of rights and liberties we've built over decades. Like "disapply", "notwithstanding" is a Trojan horse – a subtle means of introducing profound changes under the guise of legal jargon.

"Words are seeds that do more than blow around. They land in our hearts and not the ground. Be careful what you plant and careful what you say. You might have to eat what you planted one day." - Unknown

These words, "disapply" and "notwithstanding", represent a monumental shift in how the government views and interacts with the law. They signal a willingness to push the boundaries of executive power, to reshape the legal framework to suit political ends. This is not just a matter of semantics; it's a matter of safeguarding the principles of democracy and the rule of law.

It's crucial to understand the gravity hidden behind these words. They are not just legal terms; they are potential tools for undermining the democratic process. They signify a move towards a governance model where rights are not inalienable but conditional, subject to the whims of those in power. This is a dangerous game, one that flirts with authoritarianism and risks unravelling the fabric of our democratic society.

In essence, the careless or strategic use of words like "disapply" and "notwithstanding" in political discourse should alarm us all. They may be single words, but their impact can be vast, echoing through the corridors of power and potentially altering the course of our nation's history. It's a stark reminder that in the world of politics, words are not just words; they are weapons that can defend or destroy the very essence of our democracy.

The Weight Of Words In Our Political Discourse

In the tumultuous arena of politics, words are far more than mere vessels of communication. They are the swords and shields in the battle of ideologies, the architects of our social and legal landscapes. The recent discourse in the Commons, peppered with terms like "illegal migrants," "disapply," and "notwithstanding," is not just a matter of rhetorical flourish. It's a dangerous game that plays with the foundational principles of our democracy and human rights.

When politicians like Mr. Jenrick label desperate refugees and asylum seekers as "illegal migrants," they are not just misusing terminology; they are actively reshaping public perception, casting vulnerable individuals as lawbreakers and threats. This isn't just careless language; it's a calculated move to stoke fear and division, to paint a narrative that justifies draconian policies under the guise of protecting national security.

Similarly, the words "disapply" and

"notwithstanding," as used by Mr. Clarke and Ms. Braverman, might seem innocuous, even trivial in isolation. But in the context of human rights and democratic norms, they represent a potential unravelling of the legal fabric that protects us all. These words are not mere legal jargon; they are the thin end of a wedge that could split apart our society's commitment to fairness, justice, and the rule of law.

This is not a battle of semantics. It's a struggle for the soul of our nation, where the words we choose and the context in which we use them have profound implications. As politicians wield these terms with reckless abandon, it's imperative that we, as citizens, stay vigilant. We must scrutinize the language used by our leaders, understanding that each word, each phrase, carries the weight of history and the power to shape our future.

The recent comments in the Commons serve as a stark reminder of the responsibility that comes with public discourse. The words we use can either uphold the principles of democracy and human rights or erode them. As we navigate these challenging times, let's choose our words wisely, aware of their impact and the legacy they leave behind. For in the end, the story of our society will be told not just through the actions we take, but also through the language we use to justify, condemn, or inspire those actions.

HANCOCK IN FOCUS: A PANDEMIC STORY OF MISSTEPS, MISSED CHANCES AND MISSING EVIDENCE

Unravelling the Tangled Legacy of Matt Hancock's Tenure During the COVID Crisis in Light of Recent Evidence presented at the COVID Inquiry on 30 November

As the COVID inquiry continues under the steely gaze of Lady Hallett, slicing through the usual political bullshit and monumental cock-ups of the recent past, all eyes were on Matt Hancock yesterday, the man who was running the show as Health Secretary when the pandemic hit the fan. This testimony has been on everyone's radar, with many waiting to see if he'd own up or just spin yet another wearisome yarn. Well, we have our answer. Hancock's time in office was an absolute clusterfuck of dubious decisions and gaping gaps between what he said and what actually went down. This inquiry's our chance to cut through the crap and see what his role really was in this shitshow that's left a permanent scar on the nation.

Hancock's stint during the pandemic was like a badly written soap opera with him playing the role of heroic and misunderstood Lothario. From the *'Pandemic Diaries'*, which seemed like a half-arsed attempt at covering his arse, to the baffling choices that left everyone asking, *"What the actual fuck?"*, his actions have been under the microscope. As he steps up to the plate, it's not just about what he did or didn't do - it's a reflection of the government's fumbling in the face of a crisis that brought the country to its knees.

Background On Hancock's Tenure

Before we dive into the meat of Hancock's performance at the inquiry, let's set the stage with a bit of background on his time as Health Secretary. It was like watching a someone carving up a turkey with a sledgehammer. Hancock landed this gig, and boom - along comes COVID-19, turning the world upside down. You'd think this was his moment to step up, but oh boy, did he spectacularly fail to deliver (not that you would know this from looking at his evidence).

Right from the get-go, it was clear the government, with Hancock at the helm, was more about winging it than having a solid plan. We saw a string of decisions that seemed more like shots in the dark than informed choices. Remember the whole herd immunity debacle? That was just the tip of the incompetence iceberg. The government's response was less about science and more about guesswork, with Hancock leading the charge, looking as lost as a fart in a perfume shop.

And then there were the daily briefings - Hancock front and centre, dishing out half-truths and often straight-up bullshit. It was a circus, with Hancock playing the ringmaster, trying to keep the public in the dark about how deep in the shit we actually were. The PPE fiasco? A prime example. Nurses and doctors were out there in bin bags, for Christ's sake, while Hancock was up there, telling us everything was under control.

During his tenure, it wasn't just about what Hancock did; it was about what he didn't do. Testing? A complete omnishambles. Protecting care homes? A fucking disaster. Every step of the way, it felt like Hancock was just making it up as he went along, leaving a trail of chaos and confusion. And through it all, he had this knack for avoiding straight answers like they were the plague.

So, yesterday, when Hancock rocked up at the inquiry, expectations were already in the gutter. We'd seen his song and dance for months - now it was time to see if he'd stick to his guns or try a new tune.

The Pandemic Diaries Controversy

Now, let's talk about Hancock's so-called *"Pandemic Diaries."* Picture this: the country's in the grip of the worst health crisis in a century, and what does our man Hancock decide to do? Write a bloody book, that's what. But here's the crux – these *"diaries"* were penned after the whole damn thing had unfolded. That's right, a post-facto scramble to rewrite history, like painting lipstick on a pig and calling it your good friend Phyllis.

These diaries were meant to be Hancock's inside scoop, his view from the trenches. But instead, they came off more like a kid caught with his hand in the cookie jar, frantically making up excuses. He teamed up with *"journalist"* Isabel Oakeshott, and together they tried to spin this narrative that somehow, in the midst of all the fuck-ups and fiascos, Hancock was the unsung hero, the brains of the operation. Talk about a delusional daydream.

When Hancock trotted out these diaries at the inquiry, Hugo Keith, was having none of it. Keith is not a man to suffer fools, and he went straight for the jugular. He got Hancock to admit that these so-called diaries weren't even written as events happened, but cobbled together later, like some shoddy patchwork of afterthoughts and revisions. It was a moment of pure theatre, watching Hancock squirm as Keith tore through the façade of these diaries, revealing them for what they were: a desperate attempt to salvage a legacy that was already going down in flames.

The whole diary fiasco spoke volumes about Hancock's approach to the pandemic. Instead of being upfront and owning his shit, he tried to rewrite the narrative, to turn himself from the villain of the piece into some sort of tragic hero. But all he really did was further cement his reputation as a man more concerned with his own image than the harsh reality of the crisis he was supposed to be managing.

The Lockdown Claim And Its

Implications

Then comes Hancock's bombshell claim - that he was the lone voice in the wilderness, advocating for an early lockdown in March 2020. It's like he expects us to believe he was some sort of lockdown crusader, bravely fighting against the tide. But hold on, why wasn't this little nugget in his so-called diaries? Oh, that's right, because it's a steaming pile of after-the-fact bullshit.

In the diaries, this crucial piece of information is conspicuously absent, like it just slipped his mind while he was busy painting himself as the hero in his revisionist fantasy. And when pressed for proof during the inquiry, what does our man Hancock offer? A hazy recollection. That's it. No evidence, no records, just a convenient memory that surfaces at the perfect moment to make him look good. If that's not a flaccid attempt in arse-covering, I don't know what is.

This glaring omission and the flimsy nature of his *'evidence'* is a bloody insult to anyone paying attention. It reeks of Hancock trying to retrofit his actions to fit the narrative he wants us to buy - that he was the good guy in all this chaos. It's a slapdash attempt to rewrite history, but all it really does is erode whatever shreds of credibility he had left.

This lockdown claim is more than just Hancock trying to save face; it's indicative of the entire government's pandemic strategy - a haphazard, make-it-up-as-you-go approach, where decisions seemed to be based more on political convenience than on hard facts or scientific advice. Hancock's retrospective heroism is a microcosm of the government's broader failure to handle the pandemic with the seriousness and foresight it demanded.

Hancock's lockdown claim, with its conspicuous absence from his diaries and the lack of any real proof, doesn't just undermine his credibility - it's a damning indictment of the government's overall strategy during the pandemic. It paints a picture of a government more concerned with managing PR than managing a public health crisis.

The Whatsapp Chats And Government Dynamics

Now, let's dive into the cosy little WhatsApp chats between Hancock and Boris Johnson. These gems, revealed during the inquiry, were like a peek behind the curtain, showing us the real script while the country was being fed a different story altogether. These chats weren't just chit-chat; they were a window into the complacent, almost farcical attitude at the heart of the government's pandemic response.

In these messages, there's Hancock and Johnson, patting each other on the back, all buddy-buddy, while the country was spiralling into a full-blown health crisis. Hancock, ever the eager beaver, is pitching ideas like a national hand-washing campaign, while Johnson's responses are about as committed as a cat at a dog show. “Ok let’s talk mon. Am off to rugby,” replies Johnson, as if planning pandemic responses was less pressing than a weekend scrum. It’s like watching a parody, except it’s real life, and people are dying.

These chats starkly contrast with the public persona and statements both were putting out at the time. On TV, they were all solemn faces and grave tones, talking about taking decisive action. But on WhatsApp? It’s like a scene from a bloody sitcom. The disconnect is staggering. It’s like they were playing two different roles: one for the public, all serious and leader-like, and another in private, where it seemed like a bit of a laugh, a casual banter session between pals.

This two-faced approach wasn't just a bad look; it was downright dangerous. While the public was being told to brace for impact, Hancock and Johnson were seemingly treating the pandemic response like a bothersome chore. It's this kind of attitude that led to delayed decisions, mixed messages, and ultimately, a botched handling of a crisis that cost thousands of lives.

The WhatsApp chats between Hancock and Johnson lay bare the jarring disparity between their public statements and their private attitudes during key moments of the pandemic. This duality in their approach didn't just undermine public trust; it was emblematic of a government that seemed to be winging it, even in the face of an unprecedented national emergency.

Shifting The Blame: The "Toxic Culture" Defence

When backed into a corner, Hancock played the blame game, pointing fingers at what he called the *"toxic culture"* in No. 10. His favourite scapegoat? Dominic Cummings. It was like watching a schoolboy trying to dodge detention by ratting out his mate. Hancock spun this tale of being the lone soldier, battling against the chaos created by Cummings and others in the heart of government. According to him, he was trying to steer the ship while others were busy drilling holes in it.

This defence is about as stable as a unicycle on an ice rink. Blaming the toxic culture for his own failings? Come on, that's a bit rich, even for Hancock. Sure, Cummings is no saint, but pinning the entire pandemic response, or the lack thereof, on him and the No. 10 culture is a stretch too far. It's like Hancock's saying, *"It wasn't me who fucked up; it was the environment I was in."* A convenient excuse, but not one that holds much water.

Let's be clear: the pandemic required strong, decisive leadership, and Hancock, as Health Secretary, was in the driver's seat. Holding a toxic culture responsible for his indecisiveness, lack of foresight, and mismanagement is as misguided as a student blaming their backpack for failing a test. It just doesn't quite add up.

Moreover, this defence doesn't align with the overall handling of the pandemic. It's a deflection, a way to shift the spotlight from his own shortcomings. If the culture was indeed toxic, why didn't we see Hancock taking a stand when it mattered? Why were there so many U-turns, so much dithering, and such a colossal mess in the government's pandemic strategy?

Hancock's *"toxic culture"* defence at the inquiry was a transparent attempt to shift blame and avoid responsibility. It's indicative of a broader issue within the government's handling of the pandemic: a lack of accountability and a tendency to point fingers rather than own up to mistakes.

The Sage Minutes And Eat Out To Help Out Scheme

In a staggering admission, Hancock let slip that he hadn't bothered to read the SAGE minutes at the start of the pandemic. That's like a pilot not checking the weather before a flight - it's fucking basic stuff. Instead, he relied on summaries, like someone skimming the cliff notes before a big exam. This isn't just laziness; it's downright negligent. How the hell do you make informed decisions in a health crisis without digesting the advice from your top scientific advisers? It's like trying to navigate a minefield blindfolded.

This revelation about the SAGE minutes wasn't just a gaffe; it had deeply serious implications. It speaks volumes about the government's decision-making process - or rather lack thereof. It's no wonder the UK's pandemic response was more reactive than proactive. Hancock was at the wheel, but he wasn't even looking at the road map.

Then there's the infamous *'Eat Out To Help Out'* scheme. Hancock's stance on this is about as clear as mud. On one hand, he's claiming ignorance, saying he wasn't consulted about the scheme. But then, leaked texts paint a different picture. He knew the scheme was causing issues in virus hotspots and even expressed concerns to Whitehall chief Simon Case. But publicly? Hancock kept his mouth shut, toeing the party line, not wanting to rock the boat.

This duality is completely maddening. Hancock had the chance to voice concerns, to potentially steer the government away from a policy that was, frankly, about as wise as pouring gasoline on a fire. But instead, he chose to stay silent in public while privately acknowledging the problems. It's political cowardice of the highest order, a prime example of Hancock's two-faced approach to the pandemic.

Hancock's handling of the SAGE minutes and his

flip-flopping on the *'Eat Out To Help Out'* scheme show a man more concerned with appearances and political posturing than the actual health crisis at hand. His actions, or lack thereof, contributed to the government's haphazard, often contradictory pandemic strategy, leaving the public confused and the virus unchecked.

Hancock's Legacy And Inquiry Reflection

What a legacy Matt Hancock leaves behind as Health Secretary - a grim tale of mismanagement and omniclusterfucks during one of the UK's most catastrophic periods. His stint at the helm kicked off the UK COVID response, which has to date resulted 24,812,582 COVID cases, 232,112 deaths, and though 22,954,691 have recovered, the scars remain deep and painful. This isn't just a set of numbers; it's a stark testament to a government's utter failure to protect its people in the face of a deadly crisis.

Hancock's tenure, riddled with PPE shortages, testing fiascos, and the disastrous handling of care homes, reeks of incompetence and denial. His testimony at the inquiry? A pathetic attempt to rewrite a history written in the tears and blood of hundreds of thousands. The UK, grappling with one of the highest death rates in Europe, didn't just suffer from the virus but from Hancock's and the government's half-arsed, reactive bullshit.

Each decision, from dithering over lockdowns to the half-baked *'Eat Out To Help Out'* scheme (which probably helped the virus more than the economy), adds up to a legacy of disaster. Each decision cost lives. The lives of our friends, family, colleagues and those not known to us - so many of them a needless sacrifice to the altar of Hancock's cockiness and incompetence. While Hancock tried to prance around questions and shift blame at the inquiry, the stark reality of his failures was right there in the numbers - undeniable and unforgivable.

This isn't just about Hancock's personal failings; it's a damning indictment of the entire government's approach to the pandemic. A sorry tale of missed chances, unheeded warnings, and a leadership more concerned with image than action. The inquiry, while shining a spotlight on Hancock's blunders, also throws into sharp relief the systemic fuckery that let the crisis spiral out of control.

To sum it up, Hancock's legacy is a clusterfuck of epic proportions. His time in office, marked by tragedy and missteps, serves as a painful reminder of what happens when those in charge are woefully unequipped to handle a national emergency. His testimony is just the tip of the iceberg, a snapshot of a government's catastrophic mishandling of a crisis that will be remembered and rued for generations.

EXPOSING THE HARSH TRUTHS: THE UK GOVERNMENT'S CRUEL MIGRATION POLICY FARCE

A Dissection of Inhumane Policies and the Cowardly Scapegoating of Migrants by a Failing Government

I'm taking the gloves off today because what I've got to say needs to be said without any sugar-coating. As a migrant who's been through the grinder of becoming a British citizen – at a cost that would make your eyes water – I've got a bone to pick with our government's latest immigration circus.

When I read about the new measures announced to curb migration yesterday, I was staggered. Honestly, it's a gut punch to see how low we're stooping in our treatment of migrants. And believe me, I'm not one to mince words about this.

Yes, shocker of the century, I agree with the increase in the minimum salary for migrants. It's about damn time we stop companies from taking the piss out of hardworking folks. But that's where my agreement well and thoroughly ends and my blood starts boiling.

Excluding health and care workers from this fair pay? Are we taking the piss? These are the people who keep our NHS from collapsing! And the new rules on family migration? That's a new level of cruelty – a government special, served cold.

So, buckle up. We're about to dive headfirst into this steaming pile of policy mess, and I'm not holding back. It's time to call out this government's bullshit for what it is: a cruel, cowardly, and utterly disgraceful failure. Let's tear into it.

Understanding The New Measures

Now, let's tear into the meat of these new

Home Office measures. The government's playing a tough hand here, claiming they're about to make the most significant cut in net migration. It's like they're patting themselves on the back for solving a puzzle they jumbled up in the first place.

The headline grabber? They've jacked up the minimum salary for skilled overseas workers to a whopping £38,700. That's a steep leap from the previous £26,200. And if that wasn't enough to raise your eyebrows, they've cranked up the minimum income for family visas to the same figure. It's as if they're saying, "You want to bring your family? Show us the money."

At first glance, the salary hike might seem like a double-edged sword. On one side, it looks like a move to stop companies from screwing over migrant workers with crappy wages. It's about bloody time we stopped treating these hardworking folks as second-class workers, right? This could, in theory, push companies to offer fair pay, aligning migrant wages with the UK standard. A win for fair play, you'd think.

But hold your horses. This isn't just about fairness in pay. There's a cunning angle to it – it might just force local salaries up too. Picture it: if companies have to shell out more for migrant talent, they can't very well pay their local staff peanuts. It's a sneaky way to nudge overall wages up, which, let's face it, have been stagnating for far too long in many sectors.

However, let's not start cheering just yet. There's a big, ugly catch to this seemingly bright picture – health and care workers are conveniently left out of this salary bonanza. That's right, the very backbone of the NHS and our rapidly failing care system are being told, "Thanks, but no thanks." We're talking about the people who've been busting their asses, especially through the pandemic, getting paid peanuts while saving lives. How's that for gratitude?

So, there you have it. A rise in the minimum salary that could, in a perfect world, level the playing field, but leaves out those who deserve it the most. A classic move from a government that's all about the headlines and bugger all about the details.

The Exclusion Of Health And Care Workers

Now, let's dive into this infuriating decision to exclude health and care workers from the new salary threshold. It's not just a bad move; it's a colossal screw-up that reeks of disrespect and short sightedness.

I'll be honest - I'm not just pissed off; I'm fuming. This exclusion is a blatant slap in the face to the very people who have been the backbone of our healthcare system, especially after the relentless hell they've been through during the pandemic. It's as if the government is saying, "Thanks for saving our lives, now back to your underpaid jobs while we sort out the 'important' stuff."

It's a sickening display of how little the government values these critical workers. They're essential, yes, but apparently not essential enough to earn a decent wage. It's like telling someone they're vital to a project but not important enough to be paid properly. What kind of backward logic is that?

This isn't just about fairness; it's about the devastating impact on the sector. We're already teetering on the edge of a staffing abyss, and this move is like kicking us further into the pit. How in the world are we supposed to attract and retain talented health and care workers when we're practically announcing to the world that we value them less than a bag of crisps?

But wait, there's more. It's not just about the salaries. This decision also sends a clear message to potential migrant workers: "Come to the UK, work your arse off in our hospitals and care homes, but don't expect to be treated with dignity or fairness." It's a recipe for a healthcare disaster, with understaffed hospitals and overworked, demoralised staff.

This exclusion is more than just unfair. It's a monumental blunder that undermines our healthcare system, belittles its workers, and puts the nation's health at serious risk. It's a glaring example of the government's hypocrisy and a clear sign of how little they understand or care about the realities of running a healthcare system. If this doesn't change, we're not just looking at an unhappy workforce; we're staring down the barrel of a healthcare crisis.

The Realities Of Family Migration And Increased Thresholds

Alright, let's grapple with this new, exorbitant income threshold for family visas, an absolute farce if there ever was one. Jacking up the minimum income to £38,700 is not just a tweak in policy; it's a devastating blow to families, especially those in the healthcare sector. This isn't just tightening regulations; it's effectively slamming the door shut on family migration for a vast swath of healthcare workers.

This hike in the income requirement is a cold, calculated move that reeks of elitism. It blatantly tells healthcare workers, many of whom are already toiling away for mediocre wages, that they're not worthy of having their families with them. It's as if the government is saying, "Oh, you can come over and prop up our NHS, but your family? Nah, they can stay behind." What kind of heartless policy is this?

For healthcare workers, this is more than a financial hurdle; it's a gut-wrenching choice between their career and their family. Picture a nurse or a radiographer, skilled and essential to the NHS, forced to live continents apart from their loved ones. The psychological toll, the strain on relationships, the sheer inhumanity of it all – it's unconscionable. And for what? To meet some arbitrary income number plucked from the sky?

But it gets worse. This isn't just about keeping families apart; it's a masterclass in hypocrisy. On one hand, the government is desperate for these healthcare workers to fill gaping shortages. Yet, on the other, they're putting up barriers so high that many will simply choose not to come. It's a brainless strategy, sabotaging our own healthcare system to score some cheap political points.

And let's talk about the numbers. Most healthcare workers coming to the UK start on salaries way below this new threshold. So, what we have here is an insidious, backdoor ban on family migration for a significant portion of our healthcare workforce. It's like dangling a carrot in front of someone and then yanking it away just as they reach out.

This increase in the income threshold for family visas is nothing short of a disaster for healthcare workers and their families. It's a policy that breaks families, crushes dreams, and jeopardizes the very fabric of our NHS. It's a blatant display of a government so out of touch with reality that it's willing to sacrifice the well-being of those who serve our nation the most. If this is the direction we're heading, God help us all.

The Steep Price Of Migration: Unpacking The Financial Burden

The other factor worth always keeping at the front of our minds is the staggering costs migrants cough up just to bring their families to the UK. This isn't just about filling out a form and hopping on a plane. It's a financial gauntlet that drains life savings and pushes families to their limits. And guess what? The government's latest stunt with income thresholds is just the cherry on top of an already extortionate sundae.

Let's take a page from the story I wrote a little while back. We talked about the Pereiras, remember them? Their journey to the UK, like countless others, wasn't a walk in the park. It was a wallet-thinning marathon, riddled with fees that would make anyone's head spin. We're talking about thousands – no, tens of thousands – of pounds, all for the privilege of contributing to British society. And this isn't loose change; it's life-altering amounts of money.

Think about it. Visa application fees, health surcharges, English tests – the list goes on. These aren't nominal fees; they're hefty sums that add up to an eye-watering total. For the Pereira family, it was a financial odyssey amounting to over £44,000. That's right, £44,000 just to live and work here, without a penny in public funds or benefits. And let's not even get started on the lawyer fees, because, let's face it, navigating the immigration system without legal help is like trying to read Shakespeare to a toddler.

Now, with this new income threshold, the government is essentially saying, "Thanks for emptying your pockets, but we're raising the bar even higher." It's a slap in the face to those who have already paid through the nose. It's not just unfair; it's cruel. It's punishing people who've done everything right, who've followed every rule, and who've paid every fee, only to be told it's still not enough.

This isn't about managing migration; it's about milking migrants for every penny they have and then some. It's about creating a system so financially prohibitive that it borders on elitism. It's a policy that not only drains wallets but also drains the hope and spirit of those looking to build a life here. The government needs to get its act together and realize the human cost of its policies, not just the financial figures.

The Government's Blame Game: A Bullshit Excuse For Failure

The government's recent scapegoating of migration for the shitshow that is our public services isn't just weak, it's a goddamn farce. It's a cowardly, lazy excuse, and I've written about this bullshit before. But, as usual, our government prefers playing the blame game rather than owning up to their monumental cock-ups.

Pointing the finger at migrants for the chaos in GP appointments and the housing crisis is not just misleading; it's downright absurd. It's a desperate move by a government that's utterly fucked up managing these essential sectors. Our NHS is on its knees, and housing? It's an utter disaster. And who do they blame?

Migrants.

It's pathetic.

The truth is as clear as day: our public services are in the gutter because of this government's chronic underfunding and piss-poor policies, not because of migrants. Migrants aren't leeching off our services; hell, they're often the ones propping them up. They're not causing the NHS waiting lists; they're the ones working their asses off in hospitals and clinics. They're not hogging houses; they're often struggling to find a roof over their heads.

This whole narrative is not just cowardly, it's downright disgusting. It's fear-mongering, stirring up xenophobia to cover up their own incompetence. Instead of admitting they've cocked up, they point fingers at the most convenient target: migrants.

Let's call this what it is: a desperate, scummy

tactic from a government that's lost the plot. It’s a bullshit attempt to shift the blame from their pathetic inability to manage the country’s essential services. They've made a royal mess of things, and instead of cleaning it up, they’re slinging mud at migrants.

We're fed up with this nonsense. It’s high time this government stopped their bullshit blame game and started fixing the catastrophic mess they’ve created. We need real solutions, not this pathetic, blame-shifting crap. Enough of this bullshit. We deserve a government that takes responsibility, not one that throws others under the bus to save its own skin.

A Call To Action Against Government Incompetence

So here we are, at the end of this infuriating journey through the government's latest fuckery. It's a concoction of high-handed policies and ill-considered measures that threaten to rip the soul out of our already battered migration system. Let’s be absolutely clear: this isn’t just policy; it’s a full-on assault on decency.

I’m a migrant myself, and I've felt the cold grip of the Home Office's red tape strangling my life and wallet. What I've seen unfold recently is not just disheartening; it's a goddamn travesty. The government is playing a dangerous game, one where the stakes are the lives and well-being of countless individuals who dare to dream of a better life in the UK.

The exclusion of health and care workers from a fair wage is nothing short of scandalous. It's a stark display of disregard for those who've been the pillars of our society, especially through the pandemic. It's like telling them, "You're good enough to serve us, but not good enough to be paid fairly." What kind of twisted, heartless logic is that?

And then, the hike in the income threshold for family visas. It's a cold, cruel move that tears families apart. It's not just a policy shift; it's a wrecking ball smashing through the lives of hardworking people. The message is clear: if you're not rich, you're not welcome. And if you dare to come here to work in our NHS or care homes, forget about living with your loved ones. It's an abhorrent betrayal of the values we as a nation should hold dear.

The government's attempt to pin the failings of public services and housing on migration is cowardly and deceitful. It's a smokescreen to cover their abject failure in governance. It's a convenient way to deflect attention from their incompetence, their lack of investment, and their chronic mismanagement of critical services.

What we need now is not just awareness but action. We need to call out this bullshit for what it is and demand a government that serves with integrity and fairness. This is not just a fight for migrants; it's a fight for the soul of our nation, for decency, and for the values we hold dear. It's time to stand up and say enough is enough. We cannot and will not tolerate this level of injustice and inhumanity.

It's time to hold this government to account, to demand better for migrants, for our healthcare workers, for families, and for everyone who calls this country home. We need a government that's truly committed to building a fair, inclusive, and prosperous society for all, not just for the privileged few.

Enough with the scapegoating, enough with the lies and cover-ups. It's time for real change, real solutions, and a real commitment to the people of this country. Let's stand together and demand a government that upholds the dignity and rights of all, not just the few. We deserve better, and it's high time we got it.

UNWRAPPING THE MYTHS: A HOLIDAY ROAST OF CHRISTMAS CONTROVERSIES

From Pagan Parties to Commercial Chaos – Slicing Through the Tinsel of Tradition with a Dash of Holiday Cheer and a Pinch of Irreverence

It's that time of year again when the conservative choir starts its annual carolling, crowing and general baying about the impending doom of Christmas and the round the corner collapse of society. Oh, joy. According to our so very easily outraged brethren, beloved Christmas is under siege in our modern, oh-soterrifyingly diverse society - can you imagine if someone who is gay or trans wants to enjoy Christmas in their own way. The horror, the horror!

So, in the spirit of the season, let's unwrap this Christmas cracker of a myth. We're diving headfirst into the real origins of modern Christmas – those titbits conveniently ignored by the *'Christmas is cancelled'* brigade. And trust me, we're going to dismantle this farcical narrative piece by absurd piece.

Buckle up, folks, it's going to be a bumpy sleigh ride!

Those Sneaky, Sneaky Christians

Let's roll back the clock to the pagan roots of Christmas. Yep, you heard that right – the origins of our precious 'Christian' holiday are as pagan as a druid in a forest rave. We're talking about the granddaddies of winter parties like Saturnalia and Yule. Saturnalia was the Roman blowout where everything went topsy-turvy – slaves became masters, gambling was on the menu, moral compasses spun like dreidels and so, so much gayness. And Yule? That was the Norse bash where the only thing higher than the spirits was the towering Yule log.

Now, here's where it gets clever. Early Christians, they weren't about to let a good party go to waste (and also had a staggering lack of imagination, so would very often nick other places ideas). So, what did they do? They played the ultimate switcheroo. They took these rip-roaring pagan festivals and slapped a Christian label on them. Voila – Christmas was born, but more out of convenience than conviction.

So, those beloved Christmas traditions – the gorging, the tree, the festive cheers – they're just about as Christian as I am a ballet dancer for the Russian ballet company (I am not). They're spicy pagan party leftovers, reheated for an ever so slightly more plain Christian feast.

Next time some bell-ringer moans about 'keeping the Christ in Christmas', give them a nudge and remind them they're basically cheering for 'Saturn in Saturnalia' and potentially a bit of light sodomy to go with it. That's the historical truth, no matter how much it grates like burnt Christmas pudding.

The Cash Cow Of Christmas

Now, let's wade into the commercial quagmire that Christmas has become. Forget the manger; modern Christmas is more about the cash register's 'ka-ching' than anything else. This shift from sacred to sell-out didn't happen overnight, mind you. It was a slow, sly slide, greased by Victorian sensibilities and turbo-charged by 20th-century consumerism.

The Victorians, bless their buttoned-up, syphilitic hearts, they were the ones who really put the 'mass' in Christmas. They transformed it from a modest religious observance to the full-blown festive frenzy we know today. They gave us the Christmas cards, the decked halls, and the goose getting fat. But let's be clear, it was less about piety and more about showing off those shiny new industrial-era baubles and bangles.

Then there's our jolly old friend, Santa Claus. Originally old Saint Nick – a generous chap known for secret gift-giving – he got a flashy makeover and emerged as the red-suited, Coca-Cola-swigging, global ambassador of Christmas consumerism. Santa went from saint to salesman in the blink of an eye. Now, he's less about remembering the needy and more about pushing the latest must-haves from your friendly neighbourhood megacorp.

Let's face it: Christmas today is less 'O Holy Night' and more 'O Holy Shite, look at these deals!' It's a capitalist's wet dream, wrapped in red and green, and doused in glitter. As for the religious roots of the holiday? They're buried under a mountain of gift wrap and tinsel, gasping for air like a fish out of water.

The 'War On Christmas' Charade

Now, let's tackle the ludicrous, almost laughable

'War on Christmas' narrative. Every year, like clockwork, certain conservative corners start squawking about how Christmas is under siege, about to be cancelled, or buried under a tide of political correctness. It's as predictable as cheap chocolate in an advent calendar, and just as unsatisfying.

This hoo-ha usually comes from the same people who seem to think that acknowledging cultural diversity is akin to a personal attack on their grandmother's fruitcake recipe or setting a pile of orphan's presents on fire. They whip out examples like a town favouring a *'Happy Holidays'* banner over a *'Merry Christmas'* one as if it's the first sign of the apocalypse. But, what we must always remember is that it's a political tool, used to stoke fear and resistance to change in a world that's more multicultural than ever, because deep down, if you moan about this, you're likely just a frightened racist.

So, let's call a spade a spade here. This claim is not just hypocritical; it's bloody absurd. Walk down any street from late November onward, and you're bombarded by Christmas. It's in the music blaring from every speaker, the decorations choking every store, the endless adverts for sales, and the holiday specials on TV. If this is Christmas being cancelled, then it's the most ineffective cancellation in history (which to be fair, ties in very nicely to what happens when someone is apparently "cancelled" yet we can't stop hearing from them about how they've been "cancelled").

Globally, Christmas is more present than ever. It's morphed into a universal commercial juggernaut, celebrated in countries where Christianity isn't even the main religion. It's not being cancelled; it's colonising. The very idea that acknowledging other cultures and traditions during the festive season somehow diminishes Christmas is like saying adding more toppings to your pizza means there's less pizza. It's a zero-sum game played by those who can't fathom sharing the festive spotlight.

So, when you hear the high pitched screeches of *'They're cancelling Christmas!'* remember, it's about as genuine as a supermarket Santa's beard. It's a tired tune played on an old violin that's wildly out of tune with the realities of our diverse, multifaceted world.

What's Really Being 'Cancelled'?

So, let's cut through the crap and get to the heart of this so-called 'cancellation' of Christmas. The real crux of the matter isn't about Christmas being whisked away in the night like a half-eaten mince pie. No, it's about a blatant aversion, perhaps even an allergy, to acknowledging and respecting the plethora of diverse cultural traditions that exist alongside the Yuletide season.

The holiday season, in all its glittering glory, is a time that can, and should, celebrate more than just one narrative. It's a time that has the potential to be as richly varied and multifaceted as the people who celebrate it. When we open the doors to inclusivity, we're not shoving Christmas out into the cold. Rather, we're inviting everyone to the party, making the season all the more vibrant, meaningful, and joyful.

Inclusivity doesn't diminish the holiday spirit; it bloody well enriches it. Think of it like adding more lights to your Christmas tree. Each new string of lights, representing different cultures and traditions, only makes the tree shine brighter and become more beautiful. It's about adding to the celebration, not taking away.

So, when some bloke in a suit that looks a bit like an angry potato whines about Christmas being cancelled because there's a menorah next to the Christmas tree in the town square, or because a school play decides to explore winter traditions from around the globe, remember what's really being 'cancelled' here. It's not Christmas; it's the narrow-minded notion that there's only one way to celebrate this time of year.

The irony of all this is that Christmas, in its truest sense, is supposed to be about peace, goodwill, and joy to all. And what embodies that spirit more than opening our arms to all the different ways humanity chooses to revel in this festive time?

Embracing a variety of traditions doesn't weaken the Christmas spirit; it strengthens it, makes it more universal, more welcoming, more bloody brilliant.

In short, the only thing that needs cancelling is the outdated and narrow-minded view that Christmas is under threat if it's shared with other cultures. It's high time we recognise that inclusivity is the real star on top of the holiday season.

Wrap It Up, And Slap A Bow On This Bad-Boy

So, let's wrap this up like the last present under the tree. We've traipsed through the historical maze of Christmas's origins, from its pagan roots to its commercial coat of shiny, tinsel-laden modernity. We've seen how this festive season is more a patchwork quilt of traditions than a monolithic entity owned by one group or ideology.

To harp on about Christmas being cancelled is not just daft; it's a denial of the rich tapestry that makes this holiday what it is. It's like getting a beautifully diverse box of chocolates and then whining because they're not all plain milk chocolate. The beauty of Christmas, or any festive tradition, lies in its ability to evolve, adapt, and embrace the myriad ways in which people find joy and meaning.

As we stand on the threshold of another

holiday season, let's chuck out the narrow, commercialised, and politicised bull that's been fed to us. Instead, let's embrace the true spirit of Christmas – a time for kindness, reflection, inclusivity, and perhaps a little bit of irreverent fun. A time to recognise that whether you're hanging stockings, lighting candles, or just enjoying a quiet moment, the essence of the season is about coming together in a spirit of generosity and understanding.

Let's make this Christmas one where we open our hearts wider than our front doors, where we acknowledge the many stories that weave through this time of year, and where we celebrate not just the gifts under the tree, but the diverse and wonderful tapestry of humanity that surrounds us.

In the end, Christmas is what we make of it. Let's make it a time of joy, laughter, and a celebration of all the myriad ways we can light up the darkest days of the year. To those harping about Christmas being under siege – it's high time to get off the high horse, grab a mince pie, and join the real party.

After all, isn't bringing joy to the world what this time of year is really about? Let's celebrate Christmas – and all winter holidays – in a way that honours their rich history and the kaleidoscope of human culture.

THE TUMULTUOUS TALE OF 2023: NAVIGATING THE UK'S POLITICAL LABYRINTH

A Year of Unprecedented Challenges and the Road to the 2024 General Election

2023, what an absolute bastard of a beast of a year you've been. Just when we thought we had ridden the wildest of political roller coasters, the last 12 months came along, stumbling around with the finesse of a drunk teenager promising they'd only had one beer and would never do it again. 2022 had already left us reeling with its deeply unwelcome triple Prime Minister special, the heart-breaking farewell to the Queen, a war that shredded Europe's peace, and a cost of living crisis that squeezed us tighter than a ducks arse. Naively, we hoped for calmer waters in 2023.

Oh, my dearest reader, how very wrong we were!

From the get-go, it was clear: the political shitshow in the UK was far from its final curtain. Rishi "Long-Stockings" Sunak, our Prime Miniature, kicked off the year with a list of pledges that would set the tone for 2023's political ballyhoo. His ambitious goals? Halve inflation, grow the economy, cut NHS waiting lists, and, controversially, stop the boats. A tall order, and one that was repeated so often that I ended up mumbling them in my sleep to a heartily bemused husband.

Then there's the cast of characters making headlines for all the wrong reasons. Andrew Bridgen, an MP with a penchant for tasteless tweets, compared Covid vaccines to the Holocaust, earning himself a swift boot from the Conservative Party. Add to this Nadhim Zahawi, sacked for a "serious breach" of the ministerial code over tax affairs, and we've got more drama than a soap opera. The usual cast of spunkspanglers were of course also constantly about - Miriam Cates, Lee 30p Anderson, Jonathan

Gullis, Brendan Clarke Smith and so many that it felt like a travelling circus of right wing fuckery.

The year also witnessed Nicola Sturgeon's resignation as First Minister of Scotland, Mark Drakeford standing down after decades at the helm, the UK blocking Scotland's Gender Recognition Reform Bill, and the ever-escalating tensions over Brexit and Northern Ireland, made up policies about seven bins and meat taxes, scandal after scandal after scandal, and good lord, just so much more. So, do strap in, dear reader, and dive headfirst into the chaotic, maddening, and sometimes outright absurd world of UK politics in 2023 with me.

While it's letting out its last agonal breaths, let's vivisect this beast, shall we?

Frosty Fumbles And Political Pantomimes

The winter of 2023 didn't just bring the usual chill to the UK; it brought a political frostbite that had us rubbing our hands in both anticipation and dread. Rishi Sunak, nervously steering the Tory ship, set the sails with his New Year pledges, which, let's be honest, had more holes than a Swiss cheese. His plan? To halve inflation, grow the economy, reduce debt, cut NHS waiting lists, and "stop the boats" of illegal immigration. The result? A cocktail of ambitious goals with a twist of far-fetched optimism repeated so many times that toddlers were repeating it like a twisted episode of Peppa Pig.

Sunak's pledge to halve inflation was like promising to tame a wild storm – ambitious, necessary and 100% beyond any measure of his control. Meanwhile, the economy was as shaky as a three-legged legged cow on a hot tin roof, with the government scrambling to find a balance between growth, sustainability, and competence - none of which appeared to be present neither at the start nor end of the year.

In the twisted saga of the Tories, Andrew Bridgen, the resident David Icke impersonator, decided to add fuel to the fire with a tweet comparing Covid vaccines to the Holocaust. A classic case of "open mouth, insert foot" that got him booted out of the Conservative Party, becoming the only MP for Reform until December, at which point he decided that perhaps Independence is the only way forward. The level of fuckery in this was truly astounding. .

Then we had the UK government playing the overprotective parent, blocking Scotland's Gender Recognition Reform Bill. A move as popular as a fart in a spacesuit, it sparked a legal tussle with the Scottish government, only to be shot down by the courts. This particular saga was deeply, deeply troubling - the point of devolved governments is to let Scotland, Wales and Northern Ireland get on with things without Westminster's overt interference. Beyond the fact that blocking a bill that would have made a meaningful step towards greater equal rights for the Trans community, this absolutely reeked of a pettiness that we would see repeated throughout 2023.

And who could forget Nadhim Zahawi? Sacked as Chair of the Conservative Party for a "serious breach" of the ministerial code over his tax affairs. Keeping in mind that Mr Zahawi was in fact our very own Chancellor of the Exchequer (if however briefly) in 2022, this whole saga gave new meaning to sleaze - yet somehow this government managed to dig even below that as the year went on.

On the other side of the aisle, Labour held onto West Lancashire in a by-election, their vote swelling like a victor's ego. This, combined with Nicola Sturgeon's resignation and the subsequent ascension of Humza Yousaf as First Minister of Scotland, gave us more plot twists than a season of "Game of Thrones", though with fewer bared breasts (that we know of).

March also saw Gary Lineker, the face of football punditry, nearly getting the boot from the Beeb. His crime? Daring to compare the Tory asylum plan's rhetoric to 1930s Germany - which let's face it, is hardly a stretch of the imagination with what we've seen so far. Lineker's suspension stirred a media storm fiercer than a British gale, spotlighting the government's controversial stance on asylum seekers and ended with Match of the Day not having a single presenter available to host the show.

As we wrapped up winter, the Tories looked more like they were trying to herd about 200 hundred pissed off cats than run a country. And we, the bemused audience, were left wondering what fresh hell the next season would bring.

Blossoming Blunders And Policy Pratfalls

Spring 2023 in the UK was a Tory Morris Dance of missteps and mayhem, almost comical if it weren't so damn tragic and actively throwing the country deeper into the abyss of dysfunction.

April showers brought more than May flowers; they also washed away Dominic Raab amid bullying accusations. In his stead, Oliver Dowden stepped up as Deputy PM, swapping a controversy-riddled Tory for a man so bland that he can only be described as a semi-sentient blancmange in a cheap suit. Mr Dowden has filled this role as a memory wiping device with aplomb, with not a single memory of him lasting more than 60 seconds.

See, you've already forgotten about him.

The TikTok ban, a dramatic gesture in the digital theatre of security, came off more like a desperate lunge at relevance than a well-thought-out strategy. Painting Chinese tech as the Big Bad Wolf, the Tories seemed to be reaching for the stars while tripping over their own feet.

Then there was the saga of the Windsor Framework. Sunak's Brexit deal for Northern Ireland, touted as a breakthrough, was more like trying to patch a sinking ship with sticky tape. It was a delicate dance on a tightrope of diplomacy and domestic politics, leaving everyone wondering if the PM had finally bitten off more than he could chew. It led to a particular video clip of Mr Sunak being oh so very excited about Northern Ireland having access to both EU and UK markets, leaving the rather big question of why the rest of the UK can't have this privilege? This question remains unanswered.

Amidst all this, there were the leaked WhatsApp messages suggesting Matt Hancock, the former Health Secretary, had ignored scientific advice on Covid testing for care home residents - this was not new information. In the least. It did however confirm again though that Isabel Oakeshott is about as trustworthy as a viper in a pillow case - just less endearing.

And let's not forget Boris Johnson's defiant stance before the Privileges Committee. His "I did not lie" claim over Partygate was like watching a third rate, rather wobbly magician trying to make the truth disappear into a sack filled with Lulu Lytle wallpaper and what I presume is sacks of cash that the Daily Mail had just given him. It was a performance worthy of an Oscar - a pity it didn't work, with him fucking off in the later parts of the year with the puerile behaviour fit for a disgruntled employee who had been sacked for getting caught urinating in a customers coffee.

May's local elections were an absolute bloodbath for the Tories, losing about 1,000 seats. It was a resounding slap in the face, signalling public frustration with the party. The Tories' grassroot support wilted faster than unwatered plants, painting a grim picture for their future prospects. How was it spun by the Tories? Inadequately. Woefully and somehow still framed as victory.

Spring 2023 for the Tories was a blend of farce and tragedy, a political pantomime where the actors seemed oblivious to the absurdity of their roles. The party, once a stout champion of British conservatism, now looked more like a circus, and the British public had front-row seats to this tragicomedy.

Each misstep, each scandal, was a testament to a party seemingly lost in its own labyrinth, a stark reminder of how far the mighty can fall. As spring gave way to summer, the question on everyone's lips was: What next? In the Tories' game of thrones, it seemed anyone's guess.

Scorching Scandals And Sizzling Sagas

The summer of 2023 wasn't just hot; it was a political inferno for the Tories, blazing with scandals that would make even the devil sweat. The UK, once a bastion of 'proper' conduct, spectacularly nosedived down the global corruption index. Dropping seven places, it was the most embarrassing belly flop among the world's big shots, courtesy of a series of fuck-ups and public spending scandals. The response from the Conservative Party? It largely boiled down to "Who would want to be on that stupid list anyway".

In June, the court of Appeal quite rightly put the Rwanda scheme right into the bin where it belongs - where it was promptly taken out, dusted off by Robert Jenrick, Cruella Braverman's sentient haemorrhoid, and shuffled over to the Supreme Court where the government yet again promised that no, this is not a humanitarian catastrophe waiting to happen, and yes, everyone in the country wants it, because the Daily Mail said so.

In a plot twist worthy of a le Carré novel, we had a spy scandal – yes, bloody spies in Parliament! Allegedly for China, no less. The corridors of power turned into a real-life spy game, where trust was as scarce as a truthful politician. It was less House of Commons, more House of Cards (just a slightly more shit version than either the original or the Netflix one).

Boris Johnson published his resignation honours

list, and as you can imagine, it was truly a who's who of mediocrity and cronyism. Gracing the list was a certain aide who had about as much experience in politics as I have in gymnastics (none), yet no one is allowed to report about this, talk about it or mention it. Curiouser and curiouser.

A notable name left off this list was a certain Ms Nadine Dorries, that wily temptress of Westminster's Wine Bars - in a clatter of chardonnay bottles, Ms Dorries resigned as MP with immediate effect, though not surprisingly, this took her months to finalise. A deeply upset Ms Dorries went on to pen her fictional drama called the Plot (about which she was very bemused that the media was not running it as a constant front page story).

July's by-elections were another horror show for the Tories. Labour and the Lib Dems snatched seats with the ease of kids taking candy, flipping Somerton and Frome, and Selby and Ainsty. The Tories' stronghold was crumbling, and the cracks were only widening. The only seat they managed to keep was the one departed by Boris "Lard Arse" Johnson in Uxbridge, and it appeared that their whole election strategy from there has turned into a so-called War on Motorists. Which lead us to our next debacle.

The summer heat got too much for Nicola Sturgeon, resulting in her arrest. This event was seismic, sending shockwaves far beyond Scotland. It was a political bombshell, detonating in the already explosive UK political landscape.

The season's political narrative was like a never-ending circus act. Leaders and ministers were juggling scandals and policy U-turns with the grace of a drunken clown. The Tories' summer was a relentless parade of blunders and backpedalling, making the public wonder if anyone in charge had a bloody clue.

This wasn't just a summer of discontent; it was a summer of *"what the fuck are they thinking?"* Every new revelation, every scandal, was like another self-inflicted wound in the Tory body politic. As the season sizzled to a close, the only certainty was the relentless march of controversies. The Tories seemed hell-bent on outdoing themselves in the art of political facepalms.

Summer 2023 for the Tories? A masterclass in how to turn governance into a shitshow. As autumn approached, we were left to ponder: could they possibly top this spectacle, or had they already peaked in their tragicomic opera of incompetence?

Autumnal Antics And Policy Pirouettes

As autumn 2023 descended, the UK's political landscape transformed into a hurricane of chaos and controversy, with the Tories at the eye of the storm.

August was no less turbulent. Downing Street, in a PR stunt, bombarded the airwaves with its "achievements" on migration, dubbing it “small boats week”, a move that was one of the worst PR stunts that we’ve seen in a while. But the real floating catastrophe was the Bibby Stockholm barge, meant to house asylum seekers, becoming a petri dish of legionella.

This was also the month where RAAC suddenly became part of our vocabulary after it turned out that a large number of schools were teetering on the brink of collapse due to being built with concrete that was being compared to having the consistency of Aero chocolates. Right. The person sent in to sort this out? Gillian Keegan. Her most masterful moment? A hot mic moment where she was lamenting that she had been “doing a fucking good job” and no one ever thanks her for it. So, to make sure that Gilly doesn’t feel too left out - thanks. Thanks again, Gillian. Now, off you fuck.

September’s drama was unmatched. Sunak, in a baffling move, announced a weakening of net zero policies, drawing fire from senior Tories and car companies alike. In this same speech, we were also informed that he had saved us from policies like having seven bins for recycling and that there would in fact be no meat taxes. Neither of these were ever remotely policies, leaving everyone looking at their kitchen waste in a bemused and concern way and wondering just how you would go about taxing chicken nuggets.

Cruella Braverman's declaration that multiculturalism had "failed" and her controversial take on refugee status only added fuel to the fire of rapidly rising right wing ideologies more fit for a dystopian series than actual politics. Keir Starmer's Labour reshuffle was met with a bit of confusion and bemusement, but there was definitely the sense that the illustrious Sue Gray's hand was finally being seen in the long run up to next year's general Election.

October brought more shenanigans. Sunak cancelled the northern leg of HS2 to Manchester. While in Manchester. This went about as well as you can imagine, sparking a Tory backlash, while Conservative Party conferences turned into a bizarre spectacle of right-wing rallying and conspiracy theories with Cruella Braverman sounding like she had swallowed Enoch Powell whole. The Tories, reeling from Labour's victory in by-elections in Mid Bedfordshire and Tamworth, faced a crisis, with the party being labelled as approaching "Armageddon".

Speaking of Cruella - she was rather unceremoniously given the boot one fine Monday morning when our Prime Miniature was given his spine back for the day which led to resignation letters that were positively dripping with venom, political manoeuvring that appeared to be straight out of Dad's Army. She was replaced by James

Cleverly, the man who confirms that nominative determinism is well and truly dead, who was in turn replaced by the very rapidly ennobled Lord Cameron as foreign secretary killing irony in the same fell blow.

November saw Sunak stirring an international pot, igniting a diplomatic row with Greece over the Elgin Marbles. By cancelling a meeting with the Greek PM, Sunak turned a cultural debate into an international tiff, showcasing his knack for stirring historical controversies and which was ultimately as dignified as a dog taking a rather loose dump on a newly cleaned living room carpet.

The post halloweeny month brought us another quite big shock – that Mistress of Math, Carol Vorderman was leaving the BBC. While it certainly was a loss to the great British Broadcaster, the gain was a Ms Vorderman unchained, and she has been ruffling all the right feathers since then.

Rounding out the year in December, Sunak narrowly dodged a rebellion but passed his *"Rwanda is in fact a safe place with no humanitarian issues ever, we promise, please let us send vulnerable refugees there"* bill in the Commons in a stark crossing of the separation of powers that we so desperately need as a democracy. Despite the win, there was still no clear endgame for his 'stop the boats' pledge. It was like promising to fix a leaky faucet while the house is flooding.

As for the final gong of the year clock, that was

rung by none other than Liz "The Iceberg" Truss, scurrying yet again out of her cheese lined burrow to create more unnecessary drama with, well, her gongs. We have somehow ended up in a position where we've had more resignation honours in the last year than Eurovision Song Contests, and I can tell you which one I find more entertaining.

Ms Truss's gongs were particularly irksome considering that she was in power for all of 49 days, a time in which she managed to crash the economy straight into a wall and look vacuous for 90% of the time and just plain confused the other 10%.

As winter loomed, it was clear that the winds of change were more like gale-force storms, battering a Tory party that was struggling to hold onto its frayed umbrella of power and credibility.

Wrapping Up The Year

As we bid adieu to the tumultuous year of 2023, it's evident that we've been on a political rollercoaster from the deepest pits of Hades, with us, the public, unwittingly strapped in for the ride. The Tories, in their clown car escapade, have stumbled from one scandal to another, leaving in their wake a trail of policy flip-flops and a plummeting public trust. From the Zahawi tax circus to the laughable HS2 about-face, two sets of gongs which were as well received as a cup of cold vomit and just so, so much fuckery – it's been a parade of governmental missteps akin to a 'How Not To' guide for running a country.

The Labour Party, while snatching victories in by-elections, continues to balance precariously on the edge of its own internal quagmires, occasionally wading into the murky waters of controversy and power plays. Scotland, meanwhile, simmers with its unique political brew, adding another layer to the UK's complex political landscape. The collective sentiment of the public seems to oscillate between outrage and sheer disbelief at the state of affairs.

As we spin dizzily on this malfunctioning political merry-go-round, it's painfully clear that the once steady hand of British politics, the Tories, are now playing a high-stakes game of scandal survival.

Looking towards 2024, we're not just spectators in this chaotic theatre of politics. With the General Election slated for May, it's crucial that we remain vigilant, informed, and prepared. This is not just another year; it's a pivotal moment in our history where our voices, votes, and actions can shape the future of this nation. The show must go on, indeed, but it's up to us to decide what the next act looks like. So, let's brace ourselves for the main course of this political saga, and remember: in the grand theatre of UK politics, while the actors may falter, the power ultimately rests in the hands of the audience.

So, let's raise a glass to 2023, chuckle ruefully and promise to never do that again!

LORDS OF MISRULE: UNMASKING THE FARCE OF BRITISH NOBILITY

A Dissection of Cronyism and the Urgent Call for Reform in the House of Lords

In the twisted sideshow of British politics, the House of Lords looms like a grotesque relic from a bygone era. It's a historical hangover, a reminder of times when power was the birth right of the silver-spoon brigade, not the prize of the competent or the deserving. Sure, it's shed its old feudal skin, masquerading (somewhat poorly) now as a modern, appointed chamber. But let's not kid ourselves; this is still the same old cabal, a viper's nest of privilege where titles are traded like bloody Pokémon Cards, and public service is too often a laughable afterthought.

Now, let's throw in the latest shitshow from our two most recent resigned Prime Ministers: the resignation honours of Boris Johnson and Liz Truss. These aren't just lists; they're masterclasses in cronyism and political reach arounds. Johnson's roster reads like a who's who of Tory sycophants, a carnival of cronies, while Truss, in her spectacularly and calamitously brief reign, somehow managed to dish out honours like drunken party favours. The ennoblement of characters like Lord Cruddas, Lord Lebedev and Baroness Mone? That's just the icing on this farcical cake. We're talking about a system that not only tolerates, but practically drools over the shameless mixing of money, politics, and power.

This isn't about a few rotten apples; this is a bloody orchard of systemic rot. The House of Lords, in its current grotesque form, is less a bastion of wisdom and more a parade of the politically incestuous, a shrine to the antiquated notion of elitism. Stripping away its gold-leafed facade reveals a core so misaligned with contemporary democratic values, it's a bloody miracle it hasn't collapsed under the weight of its own hypocrisy and lack of self-awareness. The question screaming for an answer: Is the House of Lords a relic desperately in need of a revamp, or is it a decaying edifice that's utterly past its sell-by date in today's political structures?

Aristocratic Anachronisms: The Lords' Tumultuous Timeline

Dive into the murky depths of the House of Lords, and you'll find a bloody historical saga that's more twisty than a snake in a hedge maze. This isn't just some dusty old relic; it's a full-blown tribute to the days when power was as hereditary as a dodgy hairline and a propensity to just not stop bleeding. For centuries, it was the exclusive playground of the nobility - a club so blue-blooded it would make a royal blush.

Then, bam! The 20th century rolls around, and someone decides it's time to drag the Lords, kicking and screaming, into something resembling modernity. The Life Peerages Act of 1958 struts in, and suddenly, it's not just about the aristocratic bloodline. Life peers join the party – appointed bigwigs who are supposed to add a sprinkle of merit (and actual skill beyond just being spawned into the arms of a waiting wet nurse) to the hereditary stew. But let's not delude ourselves, it was more like slapping a fresh coat of paint on a crumbling manor.

Cue the real game-changer: the House of Lords Act 1999. This bad boy lands like a bomb, blasting most hereditary peers right out of their cushy seats. But, and here's the kicker, it leaves a sneaky backdoor open for 92 of these blue-bloods to stick around. It's like throwing a bone to a pack of old guard dogs who won't let go.

Now, in the 21st century, the Lords is this bizarre collection of life peers, bishops, and a few hereditary hangers-on, clinging to tradition like a barnacle to a ship's hull. It's a mishmash that reeks of political cronyism and privilege, where titles are dished out like champagne at a Tory Conference, often to the chums and donors of those in power, also rather like Champagne at a Tory Conference.

The debates about the Lords are a broken record, playing the same old tunes of reform and change - it feels like we've been having a circuitous discussion for years. But let's face it, changing the Lords is like trying to teach a house plant to perform heart surgery. The place is stuck in its ways, a lumbering dinosaur in a world sprinting past it.

So here we are, with this archaic chamber, a hulking testament to tradition in an age that's sprinting towards the future. The House of Lords, in all its absurd glory, stands as a bizarre anomaly, a stubborn relic of a bygone era, refusing to let go of its antiquated roots.

Honours For Horrors: The Farce Of Political Farewells

Let's slice into the steaming pile of nonsense that is the concept of resignation honours – a tradition that, in recent times, has morphed into a shameless pat-on-the-back for political cronies. Historically, it's supposed to be a dignified nod to those who've served the nation, but let's face it, it's often more about settling political debts than honouring actual merit.

Enter Boris Johnson, the shaggy-haired ringmaster of political chaos. His parting gift to the nation? An honours list that looked more like a roll call at a Tory fundraising gala. We're talking about a line-up featuring the likes of Sean Bailey, known more for his lockdown party antics than any stellar public service, and Ben Houchen, rewarded not so much for brilliance but for allegiance.

Then there's Liz “The Lettuce” Truss, the short-lived maestro of a government that resembled less an administration than a car crash that happened over the course of 49 days. Her honours list was a masterstroke of the most brass necked audacity, akin to giving gold stars to students for setting the school on fire. Jon Moynihan, a notable beneficiary, and her campaign donor, found himself with a shiny new title, in a move as absurd as it was predictable. Her list was a slap in the face of any semblance of meritocracy, doling out honours like cheap party favours.

Slipping her honours list into the New Year's batch like a thief in the night, the Tories displayed the typical flair for theatrics and obfuscation that we've come to see especially starkly over the past 7 or so years. It's as if they hoped we'd all be too distracted to notice – a gross miscalculation. Each name on that list wasn't just a nod to political buddies; it was a blatant snub to the public, a mockery of the very idea of service and honour.

The whole resignation honours fiasco has become a political sideshow, a glaring emblem of a system that's lost its way. It's not about honouring public service anymore; it's about rewarding political servitude and loyalty. This isn't just a broken system; it's one that blatantly flips the bird to the concept of honourable public service. It's high time for a reality check, a hard look at whether this tradition still has any place in modern governance, or if it's just an outdated relic best left in the dustbin of history.

Cash, Cronies, And Crowns: Tales Of Tainted Titles

Now, let's have a look at some of the most recent controversial appointments to the illustrious House of Lords that have raised serious eyebrows in the broader public, but merely raised shoulders from our illustrious Tory government.

Lord Lebedev of Siberia - What do you get when you cross a Russian oligarch's son with the British peerage system? You get Lord Lebedev, a media tycoon with a backstory that reads like a rejected Bond plot. His dad's a former KGB agent, for Christ's sake. When his ennoblement came up, HOLAC nearly choked on their biscuits. They raised the alarm about potential Russian influence – a bloody serious concern, given the current geopolitical circus. But what did our government do? They shrugged it off like it was a minor quibble over a parking ticket, not a glaring national security red flag.

Lord Peter Cruddas – Here's a classic tale of 'money talks'. Cruddas, a bloke with more money than sense, found his way into the Lords after donating a king's ransom (£3.5 million!) to the Conservative Party. HOLAC, in a rare moment of sense, advised against his ennoblement, citing concerns about his cash-for-access scandal as treasurer. But Boris, in a move as arrogant as it was reckless, decided to toss HOLAC's advice into the bin. It was a stark reminder that in our hallowed halls of power, the size of your wallet can eclipse the content of your character.

Baroness Michelle Mone – Ah, Baroness Mone, the lingerie queen turned Tory peer. She might not have raised HOLAC's hackles, but her case stinks of the old pals' act. Her journey to the Lords seems less about her contributions to the public good and more about her chummy ties with the Tory top brass. It's a classic example of the political back-scratching that plagues our system – less about what you've done for the country, and more about who you've buddied up with in the corridors of power. Her fall from grace in the PPE Medpro scandal along with Doug "The Chipolata" Barrowman is a rather large indictment on this particular appointment.

Baroness Charlotte Owen - Shhhh. We're not allowed to speak about this one (a massive, bright neon red flag all on its own).

If the Lords is ever going to be anything more than a glorified members' club for the rich and influential, this nonsense has to stop. We need to slam the door shut on this farcical appointment process. It's high time we reclaimed the Lords from the clutches of moneyed interests and political backhanders. Otherwise, we're just spectators at a grotesque parade of privilege, where the price of admission is not your service to society, but the depth of your pockets and the reach of your influence.

Democracy's Demise: The Lords' Legacy Of Distrust

When the House of Lords starts resembling

a corrupt auction house more than a revered legislative body, the public trust doesn't just wobble – it bloody well collapses faster than a Temu supplied step ladder. Every sordid ennoblement, every title that reeks of cash or political back-scratching, is another nail in the coffin of political integrity. The Lords, once a chamber where wisdom was supposed to reign supreme, is now at risk of being viewed as a cushy dumping ground for the political elite and their rich buddies.

Let's not sugar-coat it: the shenanigans of Cruddas, Mone, and Lebedev aren't just personal fuck-ups; they're glaring symptoms of a system rotting from the inside out. These tales paint a damning picture of our political landscape, where influence and power are traded like dirty secrets, and the one with the fattest wallet gets a seat at the high table. It's a slap across the face of democracy, a sneering mockery of the notion that public service is for the public good.

The impact on the House of Lords itself? Catastrophic. This institution is meant to be a reservoir of knowledge and experience, a place where laws are dissected with a fine-tooth comb by the best minds. But now, each scandal, each headline screaming of dubious peerages, shreds its credibility. It's morphing from a pillar of wisdom into a pillar of bloody salt – a bitter testament to the decay of integrity in the face of political greed.

And the bigger picture – the trust in our whole political system? It's being torn to shreds. Trust is the damn foundation of democracy, and right now, it's as scarce as hen's teeth. When Joe Public sees the Lords as a merry-go-round for the wealthy and politically cosy, it just fuels a dangerous, corrosive cynicism. It feeds the narrative that all politicians are self-serving bastards, that the system is rigged, and the average person hasn't got a snowball's chance in hell.

The fallout from these ennoblement farces is deep and toxic. They don't just tarnish individual reputations; they corrode the very bedrock of our political structure. The House of Lords, meant to be a beacon of sagacity and prudence, is on the fast track to becoming a synonym for nepotism and cronyism. If we're not vigilant, we'll be left with a legislative body that's as respected as a con artist at a carnival – and that's a fucking tragedy for not just the Lords, but for the entire fabric of British democracy.

Ripping Up The Rotten Roots: Reforming The House Of Elites

Let's cut to the chase about reforming the House of Lords. It's like trying to renovate a crumbling mansion with duct tape – a bloody challenging task, but one we can't afford to ignore.

Arguments for Reform:

The case for reform is as clear as day. The Lords, in its current state, is like a relic from a bygone era – a musty old room where the stench of elitism and cronyism hangs heavy. It's overflowing with political appointees, some of whom wouldn't recognize merit if it danced naked in front of them. Reforming this outdated institution is crucial to drag it, kicking and screaming, into the 21st century. We need a chamber that reflects the diversity and dynamism of modern Britain, not a cosy club for the well-heeled and well-connected.

Arguments Against Reform:

But let's not throw the baby out with the bathwater. The Lords, for all its faults, still houses a bunch of experienced and knowledgeable folks, Baroness Jenny Jones being a prime example of how to do things right. It's a place where legislation can be reviewed without the frantic point-scoring that plagues the Commons. Scrapping it or enforcing radical reforms might just rob us of this crucial check on government power. The devil, as they say, is in the details.

Potential Reforms:

So, what's the middle ground? First off, let's tighten up the appointments process. No more backdoor deals or peerages for sale. We need clear, transparent criteria that prioritize expertise and public service. How about an independent body with real teeth to vet nominations? Also, let's consider term limits. No more life peers lounging around like it's a retirement home. And hey, maybe it's time to seriously think about a partially or fully elected Lords. Let the public have a say in who gets to revise their laws.

In its current form, the House of Lords is like a vintage car – mildly charming but completely impractical and reeking of a dead rat stuck in the carburettor. It needs more than a polish; it needs a full engine overhaul, a detox and a spray down with a power hose. The potential is there, but without serious reforms, it risks becoming an archaic symbol of inequality and disconnected governance. Whether it remains relevant and effective? Well, that's up to us and our willingness to drag this ancient beast into the present day. It's high time we had a Lords that's less about who you know and more about what you can do for the country. Let's make it a chamber we can be proud of, not a bloody embarrassment.

The Crossroads Of Change: Reviving Or Retiring The Lords?

In this whirlwind tour through the House of Lords' murky corridors, we've seen it all: the laughable absurdity of resignation honours, the dubious ennoblements of Cruddas, Mone, and Lebedev, and the burning need for reform. This isn't just a tale of political shenanigans; it's a stark revelation of how our venerated institutions can turn into playgrounds for the privileged.

The crux of the matter? The House of Lords, in its current state, is like a posh party that's lost its charm. It's become a cesspool of cronyism and favouritism, where titles are handed out not for public service, but for loyalty and hefty donations. This isn't just a bad look; it's a cancer eating away at the core of British democracy.

Addressing these controversies isn't just important; it's bloody crucial. If we let this farce continue, we're not just risking the integrity of the Lords; we're gambling with the health of our entire democratic system. A credible, transparent, and accountable House of Lords isn't a luxury; it's a necessity.

So, as we stand at the crossroads, it's time to decide: do we let the Lords continue as a relic of an age gone by, or do we roll up our sleeves and transform it into an institution fit for the future? The choice is ours, and it's about time we made it. For the sake of our democracy, let's hope we choose wisely.

NOTABLE TWITTER POSTS

A Collection of Notable Twitter Posts

A RESPONSE TO THE CHANNEL 4 DOCUMENTARY ABOUT RUSSELL BRAND

The Post that Started it All

16 September 2023

Christ on a fucking bike, it's like watching a godforsaken car crash in slow motion. The #Dispatches documentary hasn't even finished yet, and the usual shit show is already in high gear.

So, Mr. Brand gets exposed in a documentary,

detailing a slew of alleged sexual assault accusations, backed by meticulous and damning research. And what's the public's first bloody response? "Why didn't they go to the police?" What the actual fuck? Every goddamn time a big name gets their dirty laundry aired, out pop these wankers with their dim-witted, victim-blaming bullshit.

Every. Single. Time.

How bloody hard is it to understand? With the sheer weight of evidence, the gut-wrenching testimonies, and the sheer audacity of the accusations, you'd think people might pause and reflect. But no. The AV Crowd, Conspiracy Theorists, Right Wing Bobbleheads and Truther crotchgoblins are tripping over themselves, clamouring to defend Brand, spouting their utterly moronic drivel, and doubting the women brave enough to step forward. Utter fucking bellends.

Every "Why didn't they report it?" is another slap in the face to survivors everywhere, reinforcing a piss-poor culture where victims are scrutinised, doubted, and blamed. It's like telling someone their house is on fire and then asking them why they didn't buy better smoke alarms. Twisted logic at its finest.

How about, for once, we focus on the real bloody issue: the alleged predatory antics of Mr. Brand and the fucked-up system that props up tossers like him? But no, apparently that's too much to ask in this godforsaken madhouse we call society.

Fuck me sideways.

A RESPONSE TO MR SUNAK INVENTING POLICIES AND SETTING NET ZERO BACK BY YEARS IN ONE FELL SWOOP

Date: 21 September 2023

There's nothing quite like waking up to the smell of a toxic bin fire, and that's precisely what Mr Sunak's recent announcement on #NetZero feels like. Just another day in the trash heap of political announcements and press conferences being spoken to like a seven year old whose being told that daddy is going to live with Auntie Shirley now, but he definitely still loves us. And speaking of trash, #SevenBinsSunak surely fucking knows how to make a mess of things.

Now, I'm all for a spot of recycling, genuinely, but when Mr Seven-Bins-Sunak pulls these "never-planned-policies" out of the bin, I can't help but scratch my head in utter befuddlement.

So, we're being "saved" from policies that nobody ever put on the table? A meat tax? A flight tax? Enforced car-sharing? And here I thought my recycling duties were confusing. Turns out, they're a walk in the park compared to trying to figure out what in the actual fuck actually going on in Mr Sunak's head.

Now, for our right-wing arsetrumpets who keep gleefully asking about the EU and why us “lefties” were fine with 2035 as their zero emissions target for cars: It's simple. The EU set a clear path and didn't turn it into a shitting pantomime. Their targets? Crystal clear: 55% lower emissions by 2030 and zero by 2035.

They didn't dig through their recycling bin of scrapped ideas, dress them up, and then tell everyone they're preventing them for our own good. I'd rather deal with the mythical seven (or hell, seventy-seven) recycling bins than try to sort through the load of rubbish we're being fed. Honestly, at this point, Mr Sunak could announce that we need to separate our trash into categories of 'slightly rubbish', 'utterly rubbish', and 'straight-up lies', and I wouldn't be surprised.

Fucking bins, policies, and politics aside, can we just get some transparency, integrity and accountability for once - it feels like we're well overdue, don't you think?

But until then, cheers to sifting through the trash, Mr Sunak.

THE MASK SLIPS FOR THE FIRST TIME

An explanation about why I write what I Write.

20 September 2023

I've been asked more than once, "Iratus, why all the fire in your words?" Some might assume the person behind the keyboard is constantly livid, a storm waiting to break. But let me pull back the curtain for you: in the day-to-day, I'm the antithesis of that stormy image. Friends and family often jest that I wouldn't know how to shout even if I tried. My husband, bless him, sometimes wishes I'd just let out a scream, some raw expression of the tumult inside. But that's just not me. Not in person, at least.

Years ago, I started a blog. It was a quiet

little corner of the internet where I poured my thoughts, joys, and frustrations. Like many things in life, it fell by the wayside. Life happened, priorities shifted. But the itch to write, to share, to vent - it never truly faded. So, here I am, rekindling a once cherished hobby, albeit with a more pronounced edge.

Why the rage in my writing then? Why this glaring discrepancy?

Growing up, I was fed tales of a world perpetually on the upswing. Our generation would see advancements and experiences our forebears couldn't even fathom. Yet as I inch closer to the big four-oh, it seems we've hit a regressive spiral. The promise of an enlightened tomorrow feels eclipsed by avarice, disinformation, and a disheartening barrage of ignorance.

Beyond this platform, I grapple with an ailing parent miles away - a relationship more maelstrom than calm seas. Couple that with a job that often feels like Atlas's burden, and that ever-present whisper suggesting maybe, just maybe, I'm out of my depth.

Thus, my words brim with a fervour seldom seen in my spoken interactions. Beneath every post, beneath the scorching critiques, lies a foundation of profound love - love for a world seemingly derailing. A love rooted in the aspirations handed to us as children, the hope that by raising our digital voices, we might alter our course.

Yet, there's also an underlying heartsore, a deep aching melancholy and a lamentation birthed from a world falling short. Personal tribulations, the gulf between my parent and me, the ceaseless professional self-doubt - they all fuel that ache, and Twitter has now become a room with thick walls where I can shout as loudly as I want.

At its core, I write because words have forever been both my sanctuary and my sword. Through this medium and this platform, I vent the inner tempest, hoping to instigate change, sway a viewpoint, or perhaps ignite a kindred spirit. So, to the stalwarts who've journeyed with me thus far, understand this: beneath the ire and fervency lies a tapestry woven from love, hope, and a dash of stubborn elder millennial tenacity.

Ps. I find myself yet again in a position where I'm apologising for a novel - to those of you who have been following me over the past month and a bit, thank you for letting me spam your feeds and for some of the lovely comments and feedback that you've given - even if each one isn't responded to, every one of them is appreciated.

A RESPONSE TO THE DRAMATIZATION OF PARTYGATE ON CHANNEL 4

3 October 2023

Fucking hell, that was a torrid watch. I'm watching #Partygate on Channel 4 after my relaxing dip into the warm embrace of Bake-Off, and my fingers are practically twitching, aching to bash into the keyboard with a vigour that might just break the fucking thing. Have you ever found yourself so incandescent with rage, that your every vein pulses with an almost primal rage?

You see, not only have I been yanked from my venting escapades (and during Tory conference week!), having to contend with my own family kerfuffle over the past few days, but to come back to a screen, splashing the insidious, maddening actions of those privileged twatwaffles right back into my face? It's like they've personally spat into the wounds that we all still bloody well carry!

My own personal hell over the past years, missing births, weddings, the very fabric of life's joyful moments, ripped away, all while those vacuous, sociopathic melons pranced and preened around in their ivory towers, blissfully unencumbered by the rules and heartaches that governed the rest of us. It's a kick in the teeth, a bloody mockery, and my God, does it burn a furious fire in my belly.

I personally missed my sister's wedding, the birth of my niece, moments forever lost to the abyss, while they partied, they fucking partied.

And you know what's a right royal pain in the arse? It's not just the actions of those deceitful crotchgoblins that gets me riled up. No, it's the blind-eyed, spineless apologists, the ones that scurry out from their holes to somehow, inconceivably, defend the indefensible, that really stoke the flames of fury.

The utter audacity to place a party hat upon their deceitful brows while the nation wept, suffered, and sacrificed... and I thought, my anger had plateaued. But no, watching their sneering faces, their aloof disposition splattered across the screen, it’s apparent that the rage has not even begun to peak. There’s a fiery storm brewing, and this is one tempest that will not be quelled by weary fingers or fatigued souls.

It's far from over. Once the personal tempests subside, once the immediate fires are put out, this calamitous rage will find its voice once again, roaring louder, fiercer, unyielding in its pursuit for accountability and justice. Until then, let the smouldering coals of anger keep warm the desire for retribution. Because believe me, it’s coming. And by the gods, it will not be gentle.

Fuck. Them. All.

A COMPARATIVE ANALYSIS BETWEEN CONFERENCE SPEECHES BY SUELLA BRAVERMAN AND YVETTE COOPER

11 October 2023

In what can only be described as misguided masochism, I spent the meeting free part of my afternoon poring over the transcripts from Ms Braverman and Ms Cooper's recent speeches at their respective conferences, and fuck me sideways, it was like downing a bitter, hate-infused pale ale followed by a refreshing, effervescent chaser of hope and unity.

Our dearest Cruella, last week at the Conservative Party Conference (presumably in her usual puff of sulphur and surrounded by a cloak of cloying darkness), opted to deliver a sinister sermon of separation, a wretched display of how to systematically demonise the vulnerable, wrapped in a vile veneer of patriotic duty and Union Jack Flags.

Her policies, buried under layers of blame, bile and bitterness, point towards a Britain isolated, antagonistic, and morally bankrupt. In her world, the ills of society are the fault of the “others,” the “lefty lawyers,” and she was all but shouting "fuck off, we don't want you here!" to anyone daring to seek refuge on our shores all but shouting. A dangerous and toxic narrative wrapped in a thin veil of nationalistic fervour.

Conversely, Ms Cooper, this week, spoke of

togetherness and a shared journey towards better days. Her articulated vision, one where we build support systems rather than barriers, bridges rather than walls, recognises the broader structural issues at play and addresses them rather than lazily pointing fingers at easy targets.

Mr Starmer appears to have assembled a team of competent, passionate individuals, such as Ms Cooper, who can genuinely inspire and drive meaningful change. Meanwhile, Mr Sunak's dubious ensemble of ineptitude and self-interested shitgibbons runs the risk of derailing any semblance of a coherent narrative, propelling us into a chaotic future of divisiveness and scorn.

As we look towards an election in the next 12-14 months, these conferences serve as a demarcation point, a clear division between two starkly different futures. One path leads us towards an abyss of enmity, othering and disunity, while the other towards a potential future where policies are constructed with empathy and understanding, not spite and segregation.

While I personally am not tethered to any political party, the resonance of real, genuine passion paired with competent, forward-thinking policies cannot and should not be ignored. #Labour has certainly made an impression, showcasing a future that seems not only desirable but crucial, especially when contrasted against the Tories' venomous vaudeville of villainy.

And so we find ourselves, at a critical juncture, with the seeds of division and unity sown before us, teetering on the brink of a decision that will shape our collective future. May our choices be guided by empathy, our voices amplify reason, and our actions define a future we can all stand proudly in together.

Now, if you'll please be so kind as to excuse me, I have a desperate need to scrub my fur down after reading Ms Braverman's speech twice.

I feel very, very violated.

ABOUT BARBERS AND CLOSETS

23 October 2023

Right. I am in the office today, and mercy of all mercies - I have had a three hour in person meeting cancelled because everyone has come down with something. We all know what that something is, and I can natter on to no end about how irresponsible we're being at the moment, but let's take a rather different route this morning.

I'm about to spill the tea on a matter that's been tickling my brain more than a rogue hair in a turtleneck. It's the perilous, anxiety-inducing, downright Shakespearean drama that unfolds every time I sashay my big bear arse into the barber's chair.

Let's talk about the dreaded "Wife Chat."

Oh, yes, darlings. I've been out, proud, and shamelessly queer, if very masculine presenting queer, for more years than I care to admit. I've strutted my stuff in more Pride parades than I've had hot dinners. But, and it's a big but, there's this one closet I just can't seem to fully step out of: the Dreaded Barber Closet of Lies.

Every time those clippers buzz near my ears, rendering me temporarily deaf, the question pops: "So, how's the wife?" And, like a deer in fabulous, glittering headlights, I panic. I blurt out, "Oh, Lottie? She's just divine."

See, Lottie, my imaginary wife, is a pastry chef extraordinaire, crafting croissants into shapes so intricate they'd make a drag queen's eyeliner look like child's play. We have two delightful little monsters, Tarquin (a little rugby player, bless his non-existent cotton socks) and Penelope (wee, mouthy and loves nothing more than to pull the soul right out of our elderly, also made up, Daschund). Precocious, noisy, and frankly, if they were real, I'd be tempted to put them on eBay.

My "family" has been crafted for years now, and I could quite easily write a braindead sitcom from all the adventures we've had!

Now, you might be thinking, "Iratus, why the elaborate ruse?" Well, my friends, it's a mystery wrapped in an enigma, sprinkled with glitter. Every few years, the lie becomes too gargantuan to bear, and I switch barbers, promising myself, "This time, I'll be honest."

Spoiler alert:

I never am.

Every now and then, I toss and turn at night, drenched in a cold sweat, haunted by the fear that one day, someone will shout from the rooftops, "Lottie's a lie! The kids are a sham! And the dog? Well, the dog never even existed!". Though to be fair, none of them ever have.

As to why I do this? I honestly could not tell you. Is it because I am acutely aware that there is a man I know nothing about holding a blade perilously close to my carotid artery? Could it be because when at the Barber's I'm usually surrounded by the most suburban of suburbanites?

Beats me.

Also, if you're wondering if my dearest husband has any issue with me completely erasing his existence as soon as arse meets the faux-leather seat of a barber chair? Worry not. He does exactly the same thing.

So, my queer and gay brethren, I implore you, tell me your tales. Have you, too, found yourself weaving a web of deception in the barber's chair?

Or am I alone in my barber-induced bouts of heteronormative hysteria?

Spill the tea, share the shame, and let's navigate this hairy situation together.

AN OPEN LETTER TO MESSRS SUNAK AND HUNT

24 October 2023

Messrs Sunak and Hunt, I trust this message finds you comfortably ensconced in the plush bosom of your privileges because today, we need to engage in a brutally frank tête-à-tête. I've been dissecting the Joseph Rowntree Foundation's report published yesterday on Destitution in the UK, and to articulate that I'm incensed would be to grossly understate the volcanic eruption of fury within me.

I would like both of you to realise that the

word used by JRF is "Destitution". Not just garden-variety hardship or poverty, but an utterly catastrophic plunge into a dark abyss where humans can't even scrounge together the means to stay warm, dry, and fed. It's a state of living (if you can even dare call it that), no person in this obscenely affluent nation should ever have to endure.

And yet, here we are.

The report spells it out in stark, unforgiving terms: a staggering 3.8 million souls, including an entire million of our future, the children, marooned in destitution in 2022. That's almost a tripling of the number of children and a grotesque ballooning of the overall number since 2017. And just to nip any attempts at deflection in the bud, a jaw-dropping three-quarters of these individuals are recipients of social security.

Now, gents, gird your loins because this is where the rage hits stratospheric levels.

Your government, in an act of unfathomable and brazen audacity, has decided that this moment in time, amidst this miserable maelstrom of misery, is just about right for lifting the cap on bankers bonuses. While millions languish in abject poverty, in a state of Destitution, you're rolling out the red carpet for the already ludicrously affluent to engorge themselves further. It's a slap, no, a full-blown haymaker, to the face of every family teetering on the brink, and a glaring, neon-lit billboard announcing where your true allegiances lie.

How in the seven hells dare you fatten the wallets of the one-percenters while children are condemned to a nightmarish existence of hunger and deprivation? It transcends outrage; it's a dereliction of morality that defies comprehension. You're prioritizing the grotesque bonuses of the banking bigwigs over the basic, fundamental human needs of millions. It's a grim tableau of your government's twisted values and misplaced priorities.

And let's not conveniently sidestep the Brexit behemoth, shall we? Ever since this nation decided to leap headfirst into that calamitous farce, it seems every shred of common sense and decency got jettisoned out the window. The most vulnerable and impoverished in our society are continually thrown under the bus, while you lot are seemingly more concerned with patting yourselves on the back for "taking back control".

This report is nothing short of a scathing indictment, a blistering rebuke of your government's abject failure to shield its most defenceless citizens. It's a clarion call for urgent, immediate action, for an "Essentials Guarantee" in Universal Credit, for a radical overhaul of our social security system. It's a desperate plea for help that you damn well better not ignore.

But instead of taking this crisis by the horns

(as one would expect of a functioning and competent government), you're busy playing Twisted Santa Claus to the bankers. Instead of funnelling resources into public services and weaving a robust safety net for society, you're doling out more goodies to the obscenely wealthy. It's a spectacle of moral bankruptcy and a gross abdication of your responsibilities as public servants.

Thirteen damn years. Thirteen years you've had to make a tangible, positive impact, to yank people out of the quagmire of Destitution, and this is the legacy you're crafting? A nation brought to its knees, while the financial fat cats pop champagne corks and toast to their windfall bonuses.

Your priorities are catastrophically out of whack, your policies are a masterclass in abject failure, and it's the people, the flesh and blood citizens of this country, who are paying the exorbitant price.

It's a legacy drenched in shame, and it's high time for you to be held accountable.

A REACTION TO THE SACKING OF SUELLA BRAVERMAN

13 November 2023

Right, let's break down this absolute shitshow of a day (so far).

- Cruella Braverman, booted. Watch her like a hawk; she's as crafty as a fox in a henhouse. The political in-fighting's going to explode, mark my words. Also, let's not forget the catalyst - her saying "homelessness is a lifestyle choice" and the absolute fuckery that she's been getting up to these last week's culminating in the EDL thinking people want them in London.

- Her only statement so far, the typical "honour of

my life blah blah blah" bollocks. But oh, she teases with “I will have more to say”. Brace yourselves, it's probably going to be a steaming load of vile awfulness that could make a hyena gag.

- James Cleverly as Foreign Secretary - proving that nominative determinism is as real as a unicorn wearing arseless chaps. The man couldn't find his way out of a paper bag, let alone navigate international politics.

And here’s the real kicker:

David Cameron, yes, that David Cameron, is now the fucking Foreign Secretary. Emergency ennobled by King Charles this morning - talk about a royal fuck-up. Sure, he’s got some statesman chops, but he's as unelected as a dictator. This is a dodgy move. I dislike it immensely because it sets a very shit precedent.

- With our dear Prime Miniature Sunak also unelected, it’s turning into a bloody oligarchy.

(A little giggle on the side as I take a breath: Nadine Dorries must be absolutely bricking it. Cameron gets a fancy title after a quick nudge-nudge from Sunak, while she's left down here in the dust with us plebs. Karma's a bitch, isn't it?)

- Also, Therese Coffey walked into No. 10 today and... vanished? Maybe she’s lost in the labyrinth of Downing Street. Or stuck on the loo. Either way, does anyone really give a toss?

- Rumour has it The New Conservatives (AKA, the Gammonati) are hosting a "Suella Leadership Play" meeting. A true collection of our most rabid right - expect strongly worded and slightly offensive Twitter statements to come out soon.

Cherry on top, a bunch of my actual work meetings got cancelled - how terribly convenient. (Winks with the innocence of a choirboy)

Will keep updating this thread with the happenings as it unfolds, because let's be honest - I strongly suspect that there is still much fuckery afoot.

A REACTION TO CCHQ ACTING LIKE A SPOILT ADOLESCENT

20 November 2023

Dear CCHQ Press,

Well, isn't this a delightful little shitshow? The Conservative Party HQ's press account, displaying all the grace and decorum of a dog taking a massive, runny shit on a freshly washed carpet, has the absolute brass neck to swipe at Carol Vorderman. Accusing her of "attacking young people" for being politically engaged? That's not just pathetic; it's fucking absurd.

Let's talk about your party's track record with young people, shall we? I bet you'd rather we didn't, but tough luck, I'm going there.

Let's kick off, this is a long one.

Remember the Erasmus scheme? That brilliant opportunity for young Brits to study across Europe, broadening their horizons? Thanks to your Brexit fiasco, it's now a relic of the past. Our youth are left to enviously watch their European peers enjoy what they've been callously denied.

And oh, the state of social support - or more accurately, the desolate wasteland you've left it in. You've hacked and slashed every support program, leaving young people out in the freezing cold. Housing? It's a sick joke. Safe, affordable places to live are as rare as an honest statement in one of your campaign promises.

But there's more, isn't there? Let's talk about the student loans scheme, your diabolical plan to bury young people under a mountain of debt as heavy as the Crown Jewels. They'll be paying this shit off well into their twilight years.

And the job market? You've kept Zero Hour Contracts alive and kicking, ensuring young workers' lives are as unstable and precarious as a house of cards in a hurricane.

And let's not skip over the fact that you've

effectively barred an entire generation from living and working across Europe. You're like that miserly relative who gloats about the good old days of unlimited sweets, then makes damn sure the kids today can't have any.

Ms Vorderman? She's right on the fucking money. But rather than reflecting on your monumental cock-ups, you choose to lash out at her. Is it fear? Ignorance? Probably a bit of both. It's a disgrace to see those who should be safeguarding our future so terrified of facing the truth.

So, before you spew your next round of sanctimonious bullshit, CCHQ Press, how about a bit of self-reflection? The young people of Britain deserve a hell of a lot better than the dismal hand you've dealt them. They deserve a future where they're heard, not ignored; where their hopes are fostered, not trampled by your political fuckery.

This isn't about shaming them for engaging politically. It's about you owning up to the chaotic mess you've created. And honestly, it's high time you started fucking cleaning it up.

A RESPONSE TO MR JOHNNY MERCER ON HIS UNBECOMING SOCIAL MEDIA BEHAVIOUR

28 December 2023

Mr. Mercer

Good morning.

Let's strip away the finery here and dive headlong into this little tempest in a teacup you've stirred up. Yesterday, you chucked any semblance of dignity out the window, didn't you? My opinion of you was already not sky-high, but after yesterday, it seems to be drilling.

Your response to Carol Vorderman and Fred Thomas was like a godawful, clanging disaster in the serene temple of public discourse. They quite rightly shone a spotlight on the appalling 14% rise in veterans' homelessness under your watch, and instead of facing the music, you lobbed the mirror out the window like some sulky, petulant teenager. It's disgraceful, and frankly, I'd be lying through my teeth if I said I expected better from you.

Now, let me lay it out straight, no chaser:

Your little Twitter tantrum was like a chainsaw ripping through the fine fabric of political decency. In just a few sentences, you've happily urinated all over the Nolan Principles – those core values we expect our elected officials to uphold – treating them like an inconvenience rather than the bedrock of respectable public service. Where's the integrity? Is this what you call leadership? How does accountability factor into your below-the-belt response?

Your damned job as an MP, Mercer, is to shepherd promises to completion, not devour them like some nocturnal predator. These aren't just cold stats; they are lives, veterans who've served and are now left out in the cold. Your role was to ignite hope, warm their futures, but instead, you fanned the flames of utter disappointment and resentment.

Your comeback to the criticism wasn't just off-base; it was like using a sledgehammer to crack a nut. "No-one normal really cares about your view"? That's the kind of thing I would expect to hear from a schoolyard bully, not something I expect from a bloody Member of Parliament.

The fact remains, Mr Mercer - you swore to end Veteran Homelessness and told us to hold your feet to the fire. Well, you've failed, and now you're merely being called out for your failure. The least you could have done is face this with a shred of dignity, not the pathetic spectacle you've shown us!

You're not just dropping the ball; you're hurling it into an abyss. Leadership isn't about strutting around in the sun; it's about steering the ship through the storm. Right now, that ship is sinking, and our veterans – your crew – are the ones drowning.

In short, Mr Mercer – grow up. Quickly. Act like a grown-up. Act like a Leader.

If you're incapable of that, step aside for someone who bloody well can!

Best,

A MISSIVE ABOUT THE BALANCE OF WESTERN CONTRIBUTION TO THE WORLD

29 December 2023

You've caught me home alone tonight, meaning I have nothing but time. How lucky for you - get yourself a cuppa and sit down for a chat.

Now, let's unpack your glorified view of Western

civilisation. You're trumpeting it as the globe's saviour, single-handedly lifting billions from poverty and doubling lifespans. This narrative? It's like a shiny veneer over a rotting bench.

Ignoring the contributions of non-Western cultures in global progress is not just wrong; it's just staggeringly, arrogantly simplistic.

The disparity in global wealth and the distribution of these so-called Western blessings? Stark. The poverty reduction and lifespan increase? They're the fruits of global efforts, with science and technology from right across the world as the real contributors, not just the West.

Speaking of, let's rip open the history books and shine a light on some mind-blowing non-Western inventions that rocked the world. First up, ancient Indian mathematicians brought us the concept of zero – a game-changer in the world of maths. Imagine trying to do complex calculations without it!

Then, there's paper, courtesy of ancient China. This wasn't just about writing grocery lists; it revolutionised how knowledge was recorded and shared.

The compass? Yup, also Chinese. It literally showed us the way, transforming navigation and kicking open the doors to global exploration.

But wait, there's more!

Algebra, the brainchild of Persian genius Al-Khwarizmi, turned mathematics on its head. And although Gutenberg gets all the glory, the Chinese were way ahead with their version of the printing press, setting the stage for a knowledge explosion.

So, there you have it – a whirlwind tour of some non-Western innovations that didn't just nudge the world forward; they shoved it into a new era - but I'm not done. Now, to make sure I balance things out, here are a few slightly lesser known inventions by the western world which I think we can all agree were game changers as well.

Traffic lights, an everyday sight (when not ignored), were refined by Garrett Morgan in 1923. His three-light system brought order to chaotic streets, a simple yet profound change in urban transportation.

Consider the refrigerated truck, an invention by Frederick McKinley Jones in 1940. This critical innovation kept vital supplies fresh during World War II and transformed the transportation of perishable goods.

Then there's the safety of modern elevators, courtesy of Alexander Miles. In 1887, he introduced automatic doors, a response to safeguard against accidents, significantly enhancing elevator safety.

Your daily gadgets, equipped with microphones,

owe their efficiency to Dr. James E. West. In 1964, his invention of the foil electret microphone made communication devices more affordable and accessible.

The humble light bulb in your room, lasting far longer than its early predecessors, was improved by Lewis Latimer in 1881. His carbon filament extended the bulb's life significantly.

Finally, the computer monitor you're possibly reading this on and its processing speed are advancements pioneered by Mark Dean. His work in the 1980s and 1999 at IBM led to the development of the colour monitor and the gigahertz chip, enhancing PC capabilities.

So, let's cut the crap, Martin, and let's be crystal bloody clear.

The narrative of human progress isn't a one-sided tale dominated by Western civilization. It's a rich mosaic, with each piece, each invention, and each idea from every corner of the globe playing a crucial role. The inventions we've traversed, both Western and non-Western, underscore a universal truth: innovation knows no geographical or cultural bounds.

It's about human ingenuity, wherever it may arise. So, the next time you ponder the marvels of our modern world, remember it's a collective heritage, a testament to the shared brilliance of humanity.

ABOUT THE AUTHOR

Iratus Ursus Major

Iratus Ursus Major – not the name you'd find on a birth certificate, but certainly one that's made its mark in the realms of digital discourse. This pseudonym, reminiscent of a constellation with attitude, belongs to a voice that has become unmistakably distinct in its candour and wit.

Originating from a Southern African country, where the sun scorches the earth, and the stars tell ancient tales, this author has spent the last eight years on what is affectionately known as "mud island" – the UK. The transition from the vibrant landscapes of Africa to the often grey skies of Britain has provided a unique backdrop against which a rich tapestry of commentary has been woven.

Whether dissecting the chaotic ballet of British politics, unpacking the complexities of social issues, or offering a piercing gaze into environmental concerns, Iratus Ursus Major approaches each topic with a blend of sharp insight and unapologetic honesty. The rawness of

his writing is not just in the opinions he presents but in the unvarnished manner of their delivery.
Away from the digital battleground, the person behind the pseudonym enjoys the simpler aspects of life. A firm believer in the restorative power of a cup of coffee, a visceral rant and the understated magic of a quiet evening, he finds balance in the chaos of the modern world.
With "Bear With Me - 2023," Iratus Ursus Major ventures into the world of published books for the first time. Describing the experience as a mix of exhilaration and apprehension, he offers this collection as more than just a compilation of essays and tweets; it's an invitation to engage, reflect, and maybe even crack a smile at the absurdity of it all.

Printed in Great Britain
by Amazon

38204889R00165